"Let me hold you, Mallory," Sabin said, holding out his hand.

She stood up and flowed into his arms. His body was big, comforting in its strength against her. Yet there was no real comfort in the embrace. The heated response between them was too intense ever to be soothing. Mallory wanted him closer, and cuddled nearer. She was surprised when Sabin stiffened and pulled back a little.

"Not yet," he said thickly. "I'm trying to be romantic, to go slow."

She looked up at him. His face was flushed and his lips heavy with sensuality. "Why?"

"Because you deserve it. Because I want you to look at me like you did the Greek god who played opposite you in that scene."

"That was acting."

"Well, I want the real thing. I want it all," he said huskily.

She laughed helplessly. "And you think a romantic setting will get it for you?"

He frowned. "No?"

"Sabin, who wants Little Lord Fauntleroy when they can have the Sheikh?"

"You'd rather have me the way I am, rough edges and all?"

A faint smile touched her lips. "Rough edges can be very . . . stimulating. . . ."

WHAT ARE *LOVESWEPT* ROMANCES?

They are stories of true romance and touching emotion. We believe those two very important ingredients are constants in our highly sensual and very believable stories in the *LOVESWEPT* line. Our goal is to give you, the reader, stories of consistently high quality that may sometimes make you laugh, sometimes make you cry, but are always fresh and creative and contain many delightful surprises within their pages.

Most romance fans read an enormous number of books. Those they truly love, they keep. Others may be traded with friends and soon forgotten. We hope that each *LOVESWEPT* romance will be a treasure—a "keeper." We will always try to publish

LOVE STORIES YOU'LL NEVER FORGET
BY AUTHORS YOU'LL ALWAYS REMEMBER

The Editors

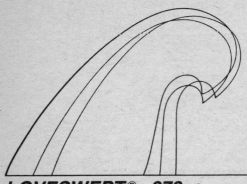

LOVESWEPT® • 378

Iris Johansen
Notorious

 BANTAM BOOKS
NEW YORK • TORONTO • LONDON • SYDNEY • AUCKLAND

One

"Not guilty."

Mallory Thane sank back in her chair, dizzy with relief as the foreman of the jury pronounced the verdict. She became vaguely conscious of the buzz of the spectators in the courtroom behind her, the encouraging squeeze of her attorney, James Delage's hand on her own, the judge thanking the jury, but it was all on a subliminal level. She was free!

James leaned forward, his intelligent face furrowed with concern as he whispered, "Okay?"

She nodded and tried to breathe slowly and evenly. She knew very well she was not at all okay. She was so exhausted and strained she could barely sit there without trembling. "Terrific. Thanks, James, for a while I thought I'd had it."

"I told you there was nothing to worry about. That damn district attorney just wanted a little free publicity to launch her new election campaign. Any other official would never have brought you to trial with such scanty evidence."

"She was a barracuda." Mallory shuddered, averting her gaze from the table across the courtroom where the sleek, commanding figure of the district attorney still sat. "I felt naked when she had me on the stand. She . . . flayed me."

"It's over now." James gathered up his legal pads and briefs and put them in his leather briefcase. "Come on, let's get out of here. We still have the gauntlet of the paparazzi to run—and fast. I intend to get you into a taxi with the speed of light."

"What more can they do to me?" Mallory asked bitterly. "They've already painted me as the premiere vamp of the eighties. Haven't you read the headlines? 'Glamorous actress seduces poor lovesick lad, leads him to the altar, accepts expensive presents, and then shoots him when he goes broke'."

"No newspaper in existence has room for a headline that long." James grinned. "And not many people have memories that long either. Next week you'll be old news."

"I hope so."

James looked at Mallory's pale, drawn face. "Look, why don't you go to Europe for a while? Give the press a chance to forget."

"On what?" She grimaced. "I still owe you money for my defense, and the offers haven't exactly been pouring in since I was arraigned for Ben's murder. I was just beginning to get a few good film roles when Ben Wyatt wandered into my life."

"I can wait for my fee."

"You'll have to." She stood and picked up her purse from the table. "But not for long. You've worked yourself into the ground to clear me, and I won't see you cheated." She shook her head wearily. "Somebody has to come out of this mess with something besides bruises or there's no sense to anything."

"Like the not-so-honorable district attorney I've gotten a lot of free publicity."

"That doesn't pay the bills when you've got a wife and a baby on the way. I'll get some kind of job even if I have to wait tables again until . . ." She trailed off. Until what, she wondered in discouragement. She had never felt so damned helpless in her life. Despite this acquittal, the press would still malign her, and she would be forever associated with scandal. Perhaps not. If Ben's murderer were caught . . . She sighed. A black widow had publicity value, but not the kind a producer believed would sell tickets.

"I'll pay you back, I promise. You've been my good angel, James." Her smile lit her face as she leaned forward and kissed him on the cheek. "It's not every day that a woman has her life handed back to her on a silver platter."

"A pretty tarnished platter," James said soberly. "That's the problem with these days of mass communication. When mud's thrown, it splatters all over the world."

"But I'm free." She linked her arm with James's as they turned away from the table and started toward the courtroom door. "Stop worrying about me. I'm a survivor. If my acting career's down the drain, I'll find another career."

"If Ben's big brother will let you," James said. "Sabin Wyatt's one of the world's financial heavyweights and judging by the way he stared at you during the trial, I got the distinct impression he wanted you locked up and the key melted down and thrown into the sea. He's not going to like this acquittal."

Mallory tensed at the memory of Sabin Wyatt's grim face in the courtroom yesterday. She had never even seen Ben's stepbrother until the trial, and yet he had been in the courtroom every single day since it had begun. That publicity shy Wyatt was willing to come out of seclusion to see his stepbrother's wife tried had served to create even more of a feeding frenzy among the paparazzi. The presence of Sabin Wyatt, one of the richest men in the world, brought a touch of mystery and golden luster, the only ingredients absent in the proceedings.

She could have done very well without those particular ingredients. The first time she had seen Sabin Wyatt across the courtroom, it had been like a physical shock. The force of his personality overwhelmed everyone around him, and she had felt panic. He had met her gaze directly, demanding her attention, demanding . . . what? She had hurriedly turned away and said something inane to James to escape from answering that demand.

There was no escape. She had felt those cool gray-blue eyes fixed unceasingly on her, and with every day of testimony she had grown more conscious of his silent intensity. She had the odd feeling he wanted her to be as aware of him, that he was willing her to be even more conscious of him than of this trial that could cost her her life. The instinct was totally illogical but then so was the compulsion that had driven her to glance at that sixth-row seat when she first came into the courtroom. She suppressed a shiver as she realized how disappointed she had been when he hadn't appeared in the courtroom today for the verdict. She should have been grateful to be free of him. Maybe these weeks of strain had turned her into one of those kooks who develop a relationship with her captors. "I've never even met the man. He and Ben weren't close and he was out of the country for the entire length of our marriage."

James looked relieved. "Maybe I was mistaken. I sure as hell hope so. You don't need Wyatt against you."

She nodded in complete agreement. Sabin Wyatt wielded more power than many heads of state, and he wasn't shy about exercising his clout. She knew that Ben had both admired and feared his step-brother. That ambivalent love-hate relationship had been characteristic of Ben, she thought sadly. "I'm not going to be around to antagonize anyone. As soon as I get back to the apartment, I'm going to pack and get out of New York."

"Where are you going?"

She smiled crookedly. "How do I know? I'll get on a bus and get off when the mood strikes me. Any place is bound to be cheaper than the Big Apple. Then I'll get a job and wait for the world to forget me."

"You're not easy to forget. That's why our eager beaver district attorney latched onto you with both hands. A chance to score with Wyatt Enterprises and a victim who has a face as haunting as the Mona Lisa's." As they moved down the crowded corridor toward the front entrance of the courthouse, James's hand protectively cradled her elbow. "You'll let me know when you get settled? Gerda will have my head if I let you go without keeping tabs on you."

She nodded. "You and Gerda have been wonderful to me. Tell her I'm sorry I can't wait to say good-bye in person, will you?"

"I'll tell her." James stopped at the front entrance and made a face as he looked through the glass doors at the long flight of stone steps leading down to the street. "Brace yourself. Your taxi's at the curb but there are three TV cameras and at least ten reporters on the steps. It'll be like running a gauntlet."

Her gaze followed James's and she involuntarily flinched. The reporters were milling around like restless tigers waiting for their prey to appear. She squared her shoulders and forced a smile. "Wish me luck."

"Always." James's hand gently tightened on her elbow. "I'll try to run interference while you go, but we may not be able to pull it off." He paused. "Remember, it's over, Mallory."

She nodded and opened the door. "It's over." She hurried down the stairs and was immediately engulfed by the questioning stream of humanity pouring up the steps.

"Miss Thane has no comment," James shouted as she fought her way through the mob. "She's very happy that justice has been done, but you'll understand the past three weeks have been a grueling experience and she's exhausted."

Mallory had almost reached the sidewalk. She pushed a microphone away from her face and ran down the last few steps to the taxi.

Gray-blue eyes glittering in a sun-browned face.

She stopped, frozen in place as the reporters crowded around her again. Her gaze focused only on the tall, powerfully built man standing beside the long, dark blue limousine directly across the street. It was the first time she had seen Wyatt standing. He was close to six five and as tough and muscular as a longshoreman. There was no earthly reason that he should look like Ben since the two men were only stepbrothers, but the contrast still struck her. Ben had been one of the handsomest men she had ever met and had had an endearing boyish quality. Sabin was totally mature, totally male and obviously made no attempt to endear himself to anyone. The bone structure of Sabin's face looked as if it had been hewn with a hatchet from a block of sandstone, yet the sheer brutal power of the deep-set eyes and broad cheekbones gave it a mesmerizing fascination. Sun streaks threaded his dark brown hair and, though she knew him to be only thirty-four, she noticed the faintest touch of gray silvering his temples.

His gaze held her effortlessly with the enigmatic demand she had become accustomed to. He was half-leaning against the limousine, his stance almost carelessly indolent, but she knew that was only a pose. Men of Sabin Wyatt's ilk did nothing without a purpose, and she knew very well what his purpose was that day.

He was here to let her know that no matter what the jury had ruled, it was not over.

As soon as the taxi bearing Mallory Thane pulled away from the curb, Sabin turned and quickly opened the door of the limousine. He locked the door in time to avoid the onslaught of reporters Mallory had just escaped. Thank heaven for the darkly tinted windows, he thought. He could see out but he knew that Carey and he were invisible to those outside. "Get out of here," he called to the chauffeur as he settled down beside Carey.

"Very tasty, that lady," Carey Litzke said. "I've

seen her on screen a couple of times in bit roles, but I didn't realize just how gorgeous she really was. Most screen stars are a disappointment in person. No wonder Ben went bonkers over her." He glanced sidewise at Sabin. "She looked pale as death, didn't she? She's had a tough time this past year since Ben's murder."

"Is that supposed to make me feel sorry for her?"

"Maybe." Carey leaned back on the cushioned leather seat. "She's been torn apart by the public, the press and the law. Don't you think that's enough?"

"No."

Carey sighed. "She's got guts, Sabin. It's a quality you usually admire. Why don't you give her a break?"

"Because she doesn't deserve one."

"You said yourself that you didn't think she murdered him. He was in debt up to his eyebrows to the mob. Your own investigators dredged up that information."

"And he spent a fortune on buying gifts for Mallory Thane." Sabin looked straight ahead. "He inherited at twenty-one, and he blew his trust fund in only three years. Where do you think he got the money to spend on her?"

"From you," Carey said mildly. "I write the checks, remember? The first six months they were married you sent him over two hundred thousand dollars. Then all of a sudden you stopped."

"I don't like to throw good money after bad." Sabin's expression was impassive. "So I told him no more handouts."

"I'm curious. Why did you decide to give him anything at all?" Carey glanced at Sabin speculatively. "You swore you were through with him after he embezzled from that account at the firm in London."

"We grew up together." Sabin shook his head. "Maybe if my father's will had divided the companies equally instead of giving the lot to me he wouldn't have—"

"Turned out to be a jealous, conniving bastard," Carey finished. "You must be feeling maudlin if you're giving away half of Wyatt Enterprises in retrospect. You know as well as I do that Ben would have run it into the ground and flitted off with the capital."

Sabin smiled grudgingly. "Probably." His smile faded. "I admit I wasn't overly fond of the bastard, but he didn't deserve to be turned into a whimpering, besotted slave by Mallory Thane. She may not have shot him, but she caused him to go to the mob for money after I cut him off."

"You don't know he gave her presents. Ben mentioned them to his friends but the prosecution never located them."

"I know." Sabin's lips tightened. "I've seen them."

"How did—" Carey broke off as he saw Sabin's expression become shuttered. He had kept both his job as Sabin's personal assistant, and the man's friendship, by knowing when to push and when to hold his peace. He valued both, and now instinct told him to back off.

Still, Sabin's entire attitude toward Mallory Thane struck him as odd. In fact, from the moment Sabin had received the first communication from his stepbrother after his marriage two years earlier, his behavior had exhibited little resemblance to the hardheaded, ruthless business man Carey knew him to be. The two hundred thousand dollars paid out in monthly increments during the first six months of Ben's marriage had completely mystified Carey. A lump sum for a wedding present he could have understood: Sabin was a generous man and the challenge of the acquisition of money meant more to him than keeping it. No, it was the way the money was given rather than the giving itself that had bewildered him. "You want Mallory Thane's hide?"

A faint smile touched Sabin's lips. "Very well put."

"Okay." Carey shrugged. "How do we go about it?"

"You're going to offer her a job." Sabin gazed out the dark-tinted window at the streets passing by. "I've set it up with Global Cinema. A small part in a low budget movie called *Breakaway*. She'd suspect anything but a minor role with an independent outfit after the notoriety she's suffered. I figure she'll jump at the chance."

"No doubt. She's dead broke according to Randolph's investigators," Carey said. "Then what?"

"*Breakaway* is to be filmed in Sedikhan."

Carey gave a low whistle. "And Alex Ben Raschid owes you a favor for helping expose that chemical warfare plant in Said Ababa. The poor kid's going to be walking into a set-up."

"Poor kid?" Sabin's gaze turned icy as it shifted to Carey's face. "You seem to be as taken with Mallory Thane as my late stepbrother. Perhaps you'd rather I send someone else to bait the trap."

"I didn't say that," Carey said quietly. "I've never known you to be unfair in all the years I've worked for you, Sabin. If you think she took Ben for a ride and deserves to be taken down herself, that's good enough for me."

Sabin was silent a moment and then a rare smile lit his craggy face with warmth. "Sorry. I'm a little on edge. This thing has me tied up in knots."

"I've noticed," Carey said dryly. "You've been barking at everyone for months." Longer than that actually. Carey recalled Sabin's temper had been uncertain since he'd received Ben's first letter after his marriage. "Randolph's last report said she'd sublet her apartment effective next week, but my bet is that she's going to leave town as soon as possible. If you want her right away, I'd better move fast."

"Oh, yes, I want her right away." Sabin opened a compartment on the convenience board in front of him and pulled out a light blue jacketed manuscript and a manilla envelope and handed them both to Carey. "The script, a synopsis of the story, and the role we're offering her, contract and airline tickets, also an advance that will permit her to settle outstanding debts."

"And put her in debt to you."

"Exactly. The airline reservation is for the day after tomorrow. That will give her time to settle her affairs and yet not enough time for her to start to wonder why Global's willing to take a chance on her when no other studio is."

"Very clever," Carey said. "And when am I to deliver these twenty pieces of silver?"

"We're on our way to her apartment now." Sabin lifted a brow. "You can still back out. I've never seen you so reluctant to do a job."

"She's got guts," Carey said simply. "For the last three weeks I've been watching her every night on the evening news, and she's taken everything they've thrown at her and never lost her dignity. She may be a bitch, but you still have to admire her."

"Speak for yourself." Barely contained savagery tinged Sabin's voice. "I don't admire cheats. I only collect from them." He drew a deep breath and when he spoke again his voice was even. "Tell her you'll meet her at Marasef airport. We'll take the Lear Jet to Sedikhan tonight."

Carey nodded as he placed the script and the envelope in his briefcase and snapped it shut. "She impresses me as being very intelligent. She'll check with Global to be sure it's on the up and up."

"She'll get the right answer. I bought Global last week."

Carey's eyes widened. "I didn't know. Why didn't you tell me?"

Sabin smiled sardonically. "Because every night when we watched the evening news I noticed just how enthralled you were with her."

"You thought I'd betray you? For Pete's sake, Sabin. She's not Helen of Troy."

"Close enough. I didn't want to take the chance." He looked out the window again. "Is she sleeping with James Delage?"

"I told Randolph you'd inquired. He said he didn't think so. Delage seems devoted to his wife."

"I didn't ask what Randolph thought. I asked if she was sleeping with that damn shyster lawyer."

"Easy," Carey said. "Randolph said he'd have a report on your desk by five this evening."

"Good."

The limousine pulled up in front of a brownstone and the chauffeur jumped out and hurried around to open the door.

Carey got out of the car and stood in the street looking hesitantly at Sabin. "I don't suppose you'd change your mind?"

"No way. Come back to the office when you're through." Sabin's expression suddenly softened. "You're doing the right thing, Carey. Believe me, she's the kind of woman who can turn any man inside out before she's through with him."

"I believe you." Carey still hesitated. He had the feeling there was something more behind all this. "It's just hard to—" He broke off and took a step back. "I'll stop and have lunch before I come back to the office. I may need to wash the bad taste out of my mouth." He wheeled and started up the steps of the brownstone.

The chauffeur closed the car door and soon the limousine was gliding through the tree-lined streets of Greenwich Village en route to the Wyatt building.

Sabin leaned back and closed his eyes trying to control the anger and impatience surging through him. Even though he'd known Mallory Thane would be acquitted, it had been difficult waiting until the trial ended. In fact, he had assisted her defense. His investigators had turned up a piece or two of the evidence linking Ben to the mob and sent it to Delage. But knowing she would soon be free hadn't quelled the temptation to whisk her away during the trial. Such an abduction was easier to arrange than most people could imagine, and he'd wanted to be done with the waiting.

He had sat in that courtroom day after day and watched Mallory Thane face her accusers, watched her grow thinner and more finely drawn before his eyes, and felt a raging need to end it. If she was to be punished, he should be the one to do it. He had grown fiercely protective of that right in the last months.

Lord, he was acting like a nut case, he thought in disgust. She was becoming as much of an obsession to him as she had been to Ben.

No . . . in his own way Ben had been wildly in love with her, he reassured himself quickly. What Sabin felt for Mallory Thane was lust. Lust was tolerable. He could use lust, but pity and admiration were totally unacceptable.

He wouldn't think of Mallory's expression as she'd flown down the stone steps pursued by reporters. He wouldn't think of the quiet dignity she'd shown in the courtroom, the dignity Carey had so admired.

But he *was* thinking about it.

Sabin impatiently reached into the compartment which had held the script, drew out a videotape and slid it into the video recorder beneath the television screen.

He switched on the machine and smiled sardonically as Mallory Thane's face appeared on the screen. *Voila*, the magic formula. Instant lust.

But lust wasn't the emotion engendered by these first shots that showed only her face. Helen of Troy. Carey's words had been sarcastic but his own had not. In his opinion the great beauties of the world were the women who displayed not only beauty but character: Mallory Thane had been blessed with both. On the tape she was laughing impishly, her face alight with mischief. Her features were as close to perfection as any he had ever seen, but what was truly noticeable was the spirit and vitality illuminating them. The wide-set eyes were an incredible blue-violet shade framed by long, dense dark lashes, and her blue-black hair was drawn severely back from her face to reveal the startling beauty of her bone structure and then allowed to fall in a long silky mass to the middle of her naked back.

Not that he could see her back now. That would

come later when she took off the full-length ermine coat and revealed that long elegant naked spine that was more erotic than most women's breasts.

He could feel himself harden at the thought, and desire brought a welcome end to pity.

She was lying down on the chaise lounge now, carelessly showing glimpses of long legs and beautifully formed shoulders as the ermine coat fell away from them. Then, slowly, seductively she took off the coat revealing she wore nothing beneath the fur but her own glowing, silken flesh.

She smiled lovingly at the camera, and then slowly raised her hand to shake back her long hair.

Sabin could feel the heavy, hot throbbing between his legs and wondered why he didn't shut the machine off. The tape had accomplished its purpose, and he knew if he continued to watch he'd be in a fever for the damn woman.

The tape was both graphic and explicit—a woman displaying herself in the most intimate ways imaginable for her lover. Yet there was nothing obscene about the way Mallory Thane tempted the viewer. She was as natural as Eve and as exquisite as man's first dream of woman. Sabin knew every movement, every toss of her head by heart and still he couldn't stop himself from watching in fascination even though the sight of her was enveloping him in a hot haze of need.

"Lord, it's . . ." He didn't know what he had been about to mutter as he reached out with a trembling hand and switched off the tape.

It didn't help. After he reached this point, it seldom did anymore.

The scene on the tape still played out its beautiful, erotic exhibitionism in his mind.

• • •

Mallory's gaze searched Carey's lean, freckled face. "Why me, Mr. Litzke?"

"Your face," Carey said simply. "We know you're a competent actress but that's not what Global is buying. You have a very memorable look and that's what we need for this role. Peter Handel, the director, saw you on television two nights ago and said he had to have that face."

"I see." Mallory stood up and wandered to the window and stood looking blindly down at the street. Litzke's proposal sounded logical and she liked the man. At first glance his curly red hair, bright brown eyes and freckled face gave an impression of Huckleberry Finn charisma, but he hadn't been in her apartment for more than ten minutes before she realized that his charm was accompanied by a forthright manner and shrewd intelligence. " 'That face' carries a considerable amount of notoriety with it. Global's taking a chance."

"We're banking on your bad press dying down by the time the picture's in distribution."

She looked back over her shoulder. "It's only my face? No nudity?"

He looked surprised. "The film doesn't call for it."

She smiled ruefully. "The only offers I've gotten lately are for less than respectable films. I don't do porn, Mr. Litzke."

"Carey." Carey's face lit with amusement. "No porn, I promise. Though after meeting you, the idea is certainly titillating. Let me tell you a little about the script. *Breakaway* takes place during World War II in North Africa. You play Renee Salanoir, a café singer and member of the resistance movement. The film's targeted at being a sort of cross between *Top Gun* and *Casablanca.*"

"Sounds like a winning combination."

Carey's smile faded. "You don't seem too eager to accept our offer. Isn't the money good enough?"

"The money's a *lifesaver.*" She turned to face him. "The job's a lifesaver. I just want to be fair to Global."

Carey's lips tightened as his gaze slid away from her own. "That's admirably ethical but Global can take care of itself. Is it a deal?"

She hesitated. "Will the role be physically taxing?"

Carey's gaze shifted back to her face. "You're not well?"

"I just need rest. I haven't been sleeping much lately."

"Or eating either, I'd bet." Carey's gaze went over her slim figure. "Have you been to a doctor?"

"I'm fine." She moistened her lips with her tongue. "I'm not up to rough location shooting, and I don't want to get sick and force you to have to stop production."

"Stop worrying about Global." Carey's voice held a strange note of suppressed anger. "Worry about yourself." He looked away from her again. "The role doesn't call for any rigorous desert treks."

"Good, then it's a deal." She crossed the room, picked up the pen, and quickly signed the contract on the coffee table. She put down the pen and held out her hand. "I'm going to enjoy working with you, Carey."

He rose to his feet, took her slim hand and shook it gravely. "I hope you'll still feel that way once you reach Marasef."

She smiled. "I will. I'm usually a good judge of character and I think you're a man who's definitely true-blue."

"What an old-fashioned term." He dropped her hand and turned away. "I'll meet your plane and drive you to the location. I'm leaving tonight for Sedikhan. If you have any problem with arrangements, contact Global."

"I can handle everything. I've been on my own for a long time. It breeds a certain independence."

He nodded absently as he moved toward the door. "I heard you were orphaned when you were fifteen."

"Was that in the papers too?" She made a face. "I thought they'd concentrated on my marriage."

"I must have read it somewhere." Carey opened the door and turned to face her. "You're sure you want this role? Sedikhan's half a world away and its reigning sheikh, Alex Ben Raschid, is an absolute monarch. You'll find things very different there."

She gazed at him, puzzled. "Of course, I want it." She paused. "If Global wants me."

"They want you." Carey's smile was forced. "I just thought you might like an opportunity to back out. Everyone deserves a last chance. See you in Marasef."

The door closed behind him, and Mallory stood there a moment gazing at the stained walnut panels. The adrenaline that had kept her going through the interview drained away leaving only the familiar, chilling exhaustion in its place.

Litzke's offer was almost too good to be true, she thought. She now had a job, money to pay James's legal fees, a safe haven, and a nice guy like Carey Litzke to smooth her way. Maybe things were ready to take an upturn. She had always found that life moved in cycles of darkness and light, and even when things were darkest there was usually something bright to hold on to. In the year since Ben's death, she had been hard put to find that light, but now life was beginning to look more promising.

She just wished she had been more honest when Carey had asked her about her health. Her lips twisted ruefully as she realized she hadn't dared tell him what the doctor had told her last week. This job meant too much to her. She'd rest after it was done and the picture was in the can. Carey had said the picture shouldn't be strenuous and she could . . .

The phone rang on the table beside her.

She tensed, her gaze flying to the cream-colored receiver.

It might not be *him*.

The phone rang again.

She whirled and picked up the receiver and said, "Hello."

A moment of silence. Then the receiver was quietly replaced on the other end of the line.

Mallory shivered as she hung up the receiver. If the phone rang again, she wouldn't answer it. She shouldn't have answered this time, but she had hoped once the trial was over he would stop calling. But why should the caller stop now when the phone calls had been going on since the week after Ben's death?

The phone rang again and Mallory gazed at it in fearful fascination before turning away and hurrying into the bedroom. Thank God, the day after tomorrow she would be half a world away from New York. She would begin packing and keep busy and eventually the ringing would stop.

The person on the other end only wanted to remind her he was still there, waiting for her.

"It's done." Carey dropped onto the visitor's chair and glared at Sabin across the width of the desk. "She took the bait."

"You're upset." Sabin's gaze raked his face. "Why?"

"Why?" Carey asked. "Because she's a damn nice woman. Because she spent most of the time worrying whether Global was getting a fair shake, and because I felt like Judas all the time she was telling me how 'true-blue' I was."

"Did you get her to sign the contract?"

He nodded. "She didn't even study it. She thinks she's a good judge of character and I'm 'true-blue,' remember?"

"That seems to have rubbed you raw," Sabin said. "She's a good actress."

"Not that good. She wasn't playing a part." He frowned. "Look at what Randolph's found out about her. She's always worked hard at her craft, she's well liked by everyone, and before she married Ben there was no evidence of lovers or sugar daddies. I think you're wrong about her, Sabin. The pieces just don't fit together."

A smile tugged at Sabin's lips. "And everything has to fit or it drives you crazy." His smile vanished. "If I'm wrong, then we'll have the opportunity to discover that in Sedikhan."

"Before or after she gets hurt?"

Sabin didn't answer. "You're out of it. I'll send a car to pick her up in Marasef. I think you've—"

"Had a bellyful," Carey finished tersely. "You're

damn right I have. You'd better be right, Sabin, or you're not going to be able to live with yourself." His gaze fell on the paper in the middle of Sabin's desk. "Is that Randolph's report?"

Sabin nodded. "Just a preliminary one. Randolph said he'd send a complete dossier later, but this has the information I wanted. She's not sleeping with Delage. She and his wife went to acting school together."

"That must have been a big disappointment to you."

"No." Sabin's expression was shuttered as he looked down at the report. "On the contrary."

Two

It seemed to Mallory the limousine had been traveling for hours since they left the outskirts of Marasef when she finally saw the large white stucco structure looming like a desert mirage against the scarlet and lavender of the sunset sky.

It was all one would have expected of this Oriental wonderland, she thought. More a palace than a house, with rounded archways, long narrow windows shuttered in lacy fretwork, and a mosaic tiled courtyard that would have done justice to an Arabian nights flick. She leaned forward and tapped the mustached driver on the shoulder. "Is that the location, Omar?"

He smiled and nodded. "Kandrahan."

"Why aren't there any other vehicles around? Is there another site other—" Mallory broke off when she met the driver's bewildered gaze in the mirror. She was being a complete idiot. Omar spoke only a few words of English as she had discovered immediately after she'd cleared customs at the airport. The man had held a sign with her name and Global

Cinema on it, and by sign language had indicated his name was Omar and he was to take her . . . somewhere. She had gotten only a blank stare when she had mentioned Carey Litzke's name and had finally given up in discouragement. Evidently, there had been a snafu and Carey had been unable to pick her up. It happened all the time on location, and she had been too jet-lagged to fuss about it.

And it was only jet lag, she assured herself quickly. Everyone experienced this chilling lassitude after long flights.

"Kandrahan," the driver repeated as he drove into the courtyard and stopped before the double front door.

"I understood that," Mallory said, again wishing for the comforting presence of Carey Litzke. The palace seemed alien, and the stark desert both enclosed and isolated it all at the same time.

Chattering cheerfully in a tongue she presumed was Sedikhan, Omar opened the car door, then helped her out. At least the chauffeur wasn't intimidating.

She was probably being foolish, she thought suddenly. If her nerves had not been strained from the past weeks' ordeal she would have been amused and curious now, not afraid. She watched Omar take her suitcases out of the trunk and set them on the tiles of the courtyard.

No one came out of the palace to greet her. Surely there were servants or secretaries or . . .

"Kandrahan," Omar said again as he got back into the driver's seat and started the car.

"Wait!" She took a hurried step forward. "Where are you going? Why—"

"Kandrahan." Omar stepped on the accelerator,

and the limousine shot across the courtyard and in minutes was speeding down the road toward Marasef.

Mallory stared at the car helplessly until it was out of sight.

"Won't you come in?"

She whirled to face the front door.

Sabin Wyatt stood silhouetted against the lighted doorway.

Shock streaked through her, and she could feel the muscles of her spine arch like a cat sensing danger.

His Richard Burton-type voice, deep, rich, each word beautifully enunciated, affected her immediately. Not at all the kind of voice she expected after seeing Sabin Wyatt's tough exterior.

"I'd come in if I were you. The desert gets pretty cool once the sun goes down."

She took one step forward and then another. "I presume this is no coincidence, Mr. Wyatt."

"There are few coincidences in this world." He smiled sardonically. "And this is certainly not one."

"No Global Cinema? No brand-new start?"

"Oh, there's definitely a Global Cinema. It's a new acquisition of mine. And there may still be a role for you in *Breakaway*. We can discuss that at a later time." His smile faded. "As you can see, I went to a great deal of trouble to have you at my disposal."

"Is disposal the key word?" Mallory glanced out at the barren dunes surrounding the palace. "You could drop a body out there and no one would ever find it."

"You seem to be taking that possibility very calmly."

"I'm not calm at all." She moistened her lips with her tongue. "I'm tired and I'm frightened and I'm so disappointed I could howl. But I've never found any situation made better by avoiding its more unpleasant aspects."

He stood looking at her for a long moment and then stepped to one side. "Get in here and sit down before you fall down," he said roughly. "I have no intention of murdering you within the foreseeable future."

"Well, that's a relief." She climbed the steps and entered the foyer. "I wasn't sure for a moment. You practically glared a hole in me in the courtroom."

"I wasn't glaring."

"No? It looked like it to me." She turned to face him and forgot for a moment what she'd been about to say. Without the civilized elegance of the suits he'd worn in the courtroom, he looked different. Soft, faded jeans hugged his powerful thighs and tight buttocks. The two top buttons of his navy blue cotton shirt had been left carelessly open to reveal the virile brown hair thatching his chest. She forced her gaze away from his body and lifted it to his face. "Okay, let's get it over with. You think I killed Ben?"

"No." He closed the door. "I know you didn't kill Ben."

Her eyes widened in surprise. "Then why am I here?"

"Because you owe me."

"What?"

His lips curved in a mocking smile. "You're a very good actress, but you know exactly what I mean, Mallory."

"I don't owe you anything. I don't even know you."

"We've never met before, but we had a mutual contact in Ben. You might even call him a go-between."

Her hands slowly clenched into fists at her sides. "Look, I'm very tired. I'm not capable of playing games at the moment. I'd appreciate it if you'd just speak out and tell me why you've brought me here."

His gray-blue eyes glittered with a flicker of anger. "I'm growing a little weary of the charade myself. All right, let's be frank. You're here because you're to occupy my bed for the next six months."

She gazed at him, stunned. "You're crazy."

"No, I believe in the integrity of a deal." He paused. "Even if you don't."

She shook her head dazedly. "I don't know what you're talking about."

He frowned impatiently. "My bed. Anyway I want you, for six months." When she continued to look at him blankly, he turned away with leashed violence. "If you still won't be honest with me, I can't force you." He yanked a bellrope. "I'll have Nilar take you to your suite. I'll expect you in the salon in one hour for drinks before dinner. Don't bother to try to communicate with any of the servants. I made quite sure none of the staff speaks English."

A small, heavyset woman, dressed in dark green Oriental draperies, appeared in the hall.

Sabin gestured to the woman and said something in a foreign tongue before his gaze shifted to meet Mallory's. "Your bags will be brought to your suite. I hope you'll find your accommodations comfortable."

Mallory shot an involuntary glance at the front door.

"No." Sabin's soft voice was layered with steel. "There's not a village for fifty miles and by the time you reached it, I doubt if you'd be alive. The desert isn't kind to strangers."

"Then you have that in common."

"But we aren't strangers." He smiled bitterly. "At least you're no stranger to me. I've wanted you for over three years."

"I don't understand any of this," Mallory said wearily. "We have to talk."

"We have six months. I'm sure we'll get around to talking some time or other." His glance was frankly sexual as it moved over her, lingering on the fullness of her breasts.

Mallory felt a wave of heat tingle through her that was as startling as it was intense. Sexual arousal. Stark, raw, and overwhelming.

He nodded slowly as he met her gaze. "I do believe we understand each other. If you please me, you'll have an easy six months even though I'm still mad as hell. I don't like being cheated, Mallory."

"Cheated?" She pulled her gaze away from his and shook her head. "I'm the one who was cheated. Tell me, did that nice Carey Litzke know what you had in mind when he lured me here?"

His lips tightened. "You liked Carey? He liked you too. That's why I decided to leave him in Marasef. I find myself very possessive where my time with you is concerned." He inclined his head. "Until dinner."

"But we need to—" Mallory stopped. Sabin was walking away from her and was already halfway down the long, gleaming corridor.

He glanced back over his shoulder. "Wear a violet dress. I like you in violet."

He was gone, leaving her standing looking after him in bewilderment.

Nilar tugged at the sleeve of her blouse, and Mallory turned an abstracted gaze toward the woman to see that she was beckoning. Mallory followed, walking behind Nilar, trying to make some sense of Sabin Wyatt's words. It was clear she must find the missing pieces to the puzzle before she could understand any of this. Only two facts were clear: Sabin Wyatt believed she had cheated him in some manner; and Ben, as usual, was involved in her misfortune.

The latter shouldn't have surprised her. Ben had been responsible for most of the unhappiness that had plagued her for the last two years. Why should it stop just because he was dead?

All right, Sabin Wyatt was angry. But he was reputed to be a brilliant man, and she should be able to persuade him there was some kind of misunderstanding.

Brilliant, perhaps, but barbarously, sensually male. She was experienced enough to read that sweeping glance he had given her.

But, according to Ben, Sabin Wyatt changed mistresses as frequently as he did his ties. A man who had his choice among the glamorous women of the world would have little interest in acquiring another one.

Which brought her back to square one and Ben.

Nilar opened the door at the end of the corridor and gestured for Mallory to precede her. The room was lovely, large, and spacious, with white mosaic tile floors that were in exotic contrast to the turquoise velvet drapes and bed coverlet that provided the only color in the room.

Exotic. Mallory found herself shivering as she realized that word also meant alien. She was very much the alien here and more alone than she had ever been in her life.

The lassitude she had suffered on her ride from the airport had been banished with a vengeance, she thought grimly. She had those blasted shakes again. Damn, they couldn't have come at a worse time. When she next confronted Sabin, she had to be calm and confident. She *would* be calm. She would just take one of Dr. Blairen's magic fixer-uppers, and she would be able to face anything.

"You did wear violet." Sabin rose to his feet as Mallory came into the salon, his gaze traveling over the violet silk lounging pajamas she wore. "I wasn't sure you'd accommodate me."

"I thought it foolish to quarrel about such a small matter. We have more important things to discuss." Mallory stopped just inside the door. "All of this has something to do with Ben, doesn't it?"

"It has everything to do with Ben." Sabin held out his hand. "Come here. Do you realize I've never touched you?"

Mallory felt the hot color stain her cheeks. The gesture was as arrogantly, sexually male as the man himself. "Listen, I know you and Ben were brothers but—"

"Stepbrothers." He poured a cocktail into a glass out of the mixer on the tray beside him and came toward her. "And I'm sure he told you he had no fondness for me."

"He was jealous of you."

"Not of me. He was jealous of the money. Ben always wanted the power without the work." He held the glass out to her.

"You're too hard on him." Mallory absently took the glass. "He was like a charming little boy who never grew up."

He reached out and cupped her throat in his big hand. "You loved him?"

Mallory felt the pulse in her throat jump and then begin to pound under his warm, calloused palm. "At . . . the start."

His gaze narrowed on her face. "What changed the way you felt?"

"I don't—" She was oddly breathless. His hand was a sensual manacle around her throat, and she felt chained, joined to him. She had to force herself to concentrate on his words, not his touch. "I thought the little boy was only on the surface and there was a man underneath. I found out I was wrong."

"You would have left him?" The demand came with sudden hard fierceness. "If he hadn't been killed, you would have left the bastard?"

"Probably." Mallory tried to step back but Sabin's grip immediately tightened about her throat, keeping her immobile. "I don't know. He needed me."

"Oh, he needed you, all right." Sabin smiled crookedly. "You were a very valuable commodity." His grip tightened. "Or were you a team?"

"Let me go, Sabin," she said quietly.

His hand slowly fell away from her throat. "Did I hurt you?"

"No." But she still felt branded, manacled to him in some strange way. "I just felt caught."

"I know the sensation. I've felt the same way for a long time." A muscle jerked in his jaw. "I don't want to hurt you. There were times when I thought I did, but I want you to come to me willingly, Mallory."

She stared up at him helplessly. The atmosphere between them was so charged, Mallory found it hard to breathe. She had never felt like this before. The sheer sexual energy of the man was overpowering. She abruptly realized it was the same primitive force he had been exuding in the courtroom that she had mistaken for hatred. That energy was drawing her to him with the dark magnetism that had compelled her during all those fear-filled weeks.

She tore her gaze away and took a step back. "I suppose I should be flattered you've formed some sort of attachment to me, but it's really quite common." She lifted the glass to her lips and sipped the martini. "Seeing a woman on the movie screen seems to generate a certain amount of unhealthy fascination in some people." She could sense him go rigid and hastily took another swallow of her drink. Lord, she was probably saying all the wrong things. Sabin Wyatt wasn't some neurotic fan who had developed a yen.

She was also doing the wrong things, she noticed suddenly as she looked down at the drink in her hand. She wasn't supposed to be drinking. The doctor had warned her about mixing those sedatives with alcohol. She immediately set the glass down on the table beside her. "But this isn't really about me, is it? It's some dispute you had with Ben that was never resolved."

"It has a hell of a lot to do with you. Do you mean he never told you how it all began?" He smiled mockingly. "I was in London three years ago when Ben was still working for the firm, and we both attended a royal gala for *Mismatch*." He saw her stiffen and nodded. "You had a small role in the picture, and we both attended the premiere. I took one look at you, and I felt as if I'd been knocked silly. I never even tried to hide it from Ben. I intended to go backstage and get someone to introduce us, but I was called away from the theater before the picture even started. There was an emergency situation in Sedikhan that stretched on for months, and in the meantime my charming, little brother was caught with his hand in the till. I bid him a less than cordial adieu. The next communication I had from him was your wedding announcement."

"You mean you think—No! He wouldn't do that." She gazed at him in horror. "He wouldn't have married me just to take something away from you."

"Wouldn't he? Tell me, how did you meet?"

"My agent introduced us. He said Ben had been pestering him for months to—" She shook her head. It was a mistake. The room blacked out for a moment and swayed dizzily around her. What the devil was wrong with her? She took a deep breath and the dizziness receded. She had to think for a minute to remember what they had been talking about. "Ben was irresponsible, but he wasn't malicious."

"Think about it." Sabin's gaze was fastened on her face. "Lord, you look as if you're going to faint."

"I'm fine." It was a lie. She felt awful. She couldn't understand why she was so dizzy and uncoordinated at this moment when she needed to think clearly. She had to tell him what he believed wasn't true. Ben had displayed sulkiness, even rudeness on occasion, but she had never been aware of any calculated manipulation.

She heard Sabin mutter a curse beneath his breath. "Okay, maybe he loved you in his own twisted way. He told me he did. Now will you stop looking like that?"

She gazed up at him in bewilderment.

"But the bastard *stole* you. He had no right to take you from me." His voice was low and fierce, his light eyes blazing in his taut face. "And you had no right to play games and then try to cheat me."

She felt almost numb from exhaustion and the shocks she had received this evening, and that blasted light-headedness had returned. She held her head very still to keep the dizziness at bay. "What . . . games?"

Anger flared in Sabin's face as his hand gripped her elbow. "You don't recall? Perhaps we should refresh your memory." He propelled her across the room and down the hall. He threw open a door on the left to reveal the muted richness of a library with wall-to-wall bookshelves, a beige and scarlet Persian carpet, and a six-foot television screen mounted on the wall across the room. "I was saving this for later but now is as good a time as any." He gestured to a beige leather-cushioned chaise lounge across the room. "Make yourself comfortable. It's show time."

He strode across the room and inserted a tape in the video recorder beneath the television screen.

Mallory gazed at him blankly and then moved across the room and sat down on the chaise lounge. That was better. The dizziness faded, leaving only a languid heaviness in its wake. She didn't want to be here, she thought wearily. She wanted to go back to her room and try to absorb the suspicions Sabin had implanted. Heaven knew, toward the end, her relationship with Ben had deteriorated into something that bore no resemblance to the marriage of her dreams. But now, if she believed Sabin's words, she was left with nothing at all.

"No, lean back." Sabin smiled over his shoulder as he reached for the remote control. "Indulge me. It's a fantasy I've had for a long time."

What did it matter? Mallory slid back on the chaise lounge until her spine was resting against the leather-cushioned back. "What do you want me to see?"

"Something we've both seen before . . . but not together." He flicked out the light and moved toward the chaise lounge. "And I definitely want to see it *with* you. Scoot over. There's room for two. I made sure of that when I bought that particular piece of furniture."

His warm thigh came as a sensual shock against her own as he settled himself beside her within the confines of the lounge. She could hear the sound of his breathing in the darkness, smell the scent of his spicy cologne, feel the warmth of his body through the layers of clothes separating them.

"Are you ready?"

Ready for what? she wondered hazily. She wasn't ready for the sexual arousal that charged the air with electricity. She wasn't ready for Sabin Wyatt's overpowering presence and vitality. She felt as if he were sapping the strength from her body with every breath he took.

"I assume silence is assent." He pressed the remote control, and the six-foot TV screen across the room suddenly came to vivid life. "You'll recall this isn't the most graphic of the lot, but it's my own personal favorite. You managed to encompass the entire range of emotion."

She gasped as she saw her own face on the enormous television screen.

"You recognize it?" Sabin's big hand began to gently smooth her hair back from her face. "Then you remember what comes after."

She did remember. How could she forget? After Ben's death she had burned those tapes. All six of them. But here they were again, haunting her with their futile eroticism. In Sabin Wyatt's possession. "You . . . shouldn't have this," she said haltingly.

"Why not? I paid for it." His voice was thick in the darkness. "I imagine I know every curve and hollow of your body better than you do yourself. I've watched these tapes so many times I'm surprised they're not worn out. Half the time I didn't even want to watch them. They made me angry and jealous and so damn hard, it was torture. I wanted to go out and find a woman, any woman, to relieve that torture. At first, I did just that. Later, I realized it wasn't doing any good. I wasn't going to be satisfied with anyone but you."

The light of the television screen flickered on his face, and she could see her reflection in his eyes, moving, displaying, offering herself. He was absorbing her, she thought hazily. With every second that passed, every look, every touch a little bit more of her flowed into his possession.

"You're not looking at the film." Sabin began to leisurely unbutton her blouse. "You should be very proud of it. It's one of your finest performances. The tape featuring the ruby necklace has a certain pagan charm, but the ermine coat truly looks magnificent on you. Ben said you were crazy to have it."

"No, you're mistaken. I never liked it," she said dully. "But Ben wanted to see me in it."

"For God's sake, don't *lie* to me. If you like pretty things, I'll buy them for you but don't pretend to be something you're not. I can't handle that right now."

"When did Ben send you this?" Her words were slurred.

"It was the first one. Two months after you were married." He parted her blouse and looked down at her. "You're not fighting me. Are you going to be honest with me at last?"

"I always try to be honest." She should be fighting him she realized in a dim corner of her mind. He was a stranger and yet not a stranger. He was a man who knew her body intimately and her mind not at all. She was beginning to tremble. "I can't seem to think. Ben . . . I have to know about Ben. The tapes."

"Forget about Ben. You belong to me now. You

should always have been mine." His lips were on her throat. "Ben cheated us both."

His voice was so intense that it swept through her, battering down the frail resistance she was trying to erect against him.

You belong to me.

You should always have been mine.

The words had been said with unequivocal belief.

"No, I loved Ben," she whispered.

"For the Lord's sake, he *sold* you." Sabin reached out and unfastened her bra, pulling it and her blouse off simultaneously. "He made you sell yourself." He looked down at her breasts in the flickering light of the screen, and she could feel the shudder that went through him. "Funny, I can barely see you in the darkness, and all I have to do is glance at the screen to see every detail of your body. But this is *you*." He bent his head, hovering his lips over one hard nipple. "The other's a dream, isn't it?"

Yes, it was all a dream.

She snatched at the concept eagerly. None of this was real, only an erotic dream with nightmarish overtones. Sabin Wyatt couldn't have formed an obsession for her when he didn't even know her. Ben wouldn't have betrayed her like this. She could accept both thoughts, if she could convince herself none of it was real.

His lips touched her nipple, and her breath drew in sharply. Heat flowed through her in a tingling, electric stream. It was as if all the force of Sabin's magnetism had centered and exploded at that first touch.

"Sweet." His voice was low, husky as his lips pulled gently on the taut nipple. "You like this?"

"Yes." Her breasts were lifting and falling with the

rapidity of her breathing. If it was a dream, it didn't matter whether she fought or not, and she was too tired to fight Sabin. He was too strong, too certain, in this world she wasn't sure of at all. His lips were igniting fires that spread throughout her body. She unconsciously arched up to meet him.

His big hands were cupping, squeezing, releasing as his mouth took.

She moaned low in her throat, and he lifted his head to look down at her. His nostrils flared as he smiled with savage pleasure. "You like me?" He unbuttoned his shirt and pulled her close, rubbing her against the thick, wiry thatch of hair covering his chest. "Tell me how you like it," he muttered. "Tell me how to please you. I want to hear you cry out like that again."

She was on fire, the tips of her breasts burning, a heavy throbbing between her thighs. Why was she letting him do this? In some remote corner of her mind she knew there was something strange about her total surrender to him. It wasn't like her to . . . The thought faded away as the sensual haze Sabin was weaving intensified, and she became conscious only of him and what he was doing to her. Yet there was something she should know. "The tapes . . ."

He stiffened and then his lips twisted in a bitter smile. "It turns you on to talk about the tapes? Okay." His fingers moved slowly down to the naked hollow of her spine. "Shall I tell you how I felt when I got them? The letter came first, you know, asking for thirty thousand dollars. Ben said you liked expensive things and he was desperate to keep you happy." He bent her back over his arm, his teeth biting gently around her left nipple. "I sent him the money. Lord only knows why. Then the first tape came. Ben said you were very grateful and wanted to show me how the coat suited you."

He began to unfasten the snap on her silk slacks. "I expected home movies. That's not what I got, and the message at the end was the *pièce de résistance*. I didn't sleep that night." He pulled off her slacks and panties and threw them aside. He looked down at her, his gaze moving over her until it settled on the curls that surrounded her womanhood. She felt a heaviness, a tingling hotness where his gaze was resting. "This is what I thought about all night. You lying before me, like this. *Damn* you. I wanted you so much I thought I'd die. And I wanted to strangle Ben."

"Ben wouldn't—"

"Put me through hell? Oh, I've no doubt he enjoyed it very much. He had something I wanted and couldn't have unless he deigned to give it to me." He fell to his knees on the floor beside the chaise lounge and rubbed his cheek on her belly, his teeth nibbling at the soft rounded flesh. "He called me three days after I received the tape and told me you had no objection to belonging to me for a short period, if we could come to an agreement. He said he was a practical, modern man and you liked pretty things. If I sent him sizeable amounts of cash periodically, he'd send you to me for six months."

Mallory could feel the faint stubble on his cheeks on her bare stomach, and a hot shiver went through her. She could barely hear his words through the haze of heat surrounding her, and she didn't understand them anyway. What he was saying wasn't making sense. No one could be as base and as manipulative as he claimed Ben had been. She would have known, wouldn't she?

"I sent the money, and every few weeks I'd get a tape. A teaser to keep the money coming." He was standing, stripping off his shirt. "I wasn't stupid. I knew what you two were doing to me, but I kept paying anyway. Two hundred thousand dollars. Did you laugh about that with Ben?"

"No."

"I don't know whether to believe you or not." He shrugged. "It doesn't matter anyway."

He was nude now and moved to stand over her. She was suddenly acutely conscious of her own nudity, her slenderness and vulnerability, the feel of warm pliant leather cushioning her body. The flickering light played on the brawny muscles of his shoulders, his flat stomach, the dark thatches of hair on his chest and encircling his manhood. He was a figure from mythology, she thought, Vulcan or perhaps Zeus.

"I knew Ben wouldn't give you to me for six months." He parted her legs and knelt between them. "He knew me too well." He began to rub the curls surrounding her womanhood, slowly, sensuously, occasionally pressing hard with the ball of his hand. "He knew I'd never let you go back to him."

No, Zeus would never give up something he wanted. But he wasn't Zeus, she remembered hazily, this was Sabin. Not that it made any difference. Power and lightning bolts . . .

"Well, did it turn you on to know what you did to me?" His hand moved down. "Let's see, shall we?" He gently inserted a finger within her. She inhaled sharply, and he looked up and smiled. "Ah yes, you want me and you're ready. What a lovely welcome." Another finger joined the first, and he began to slowly move back and forth. "And tight. I can feel you clinging to me . . ."

His smile faded as he moved forward. "I can't wait any longer," he said thickly. "Tell me you want it. Tell me you want to give me what you owe me."

The words were easy to say when her body was convulsing with pleasure with every stroke. "I want . . . you."

"Tell me you owe this to me."

She frowned in puzzlement. "I don't think . . ." She stopped. His face above her own was intense, willing her to say the words. Perhaps, if this was a dream, she did owe him something.

Then, as if to corroborate the thought, she heard her own soft voice issuing from the television screen. "Six months. Any way you like it, Sabin." The tape ended and began to automatically rewind, leaving the screen a crackling blue void.

But she had never said those words, so that proved none of this was real, didn't it? The dream-Sabin seemed to think what he demanded was true, so why not please him?

"I owe it to you," she whispered.

"You're damn right you do." The words were rough but his mouth on her own was gentle. "Mallory, love, give to me . . ."

He plunged deep!

Her scream was smothered beneath his lips.

He raised his head. "What the hell . . ."

Her nails dug into his shoulders. He was heavy, hot, huge within her. If nothing else was real in this world, Sabin most certainly was.

But he was too still. She needed more.

She tried to move, to take.

"Be still." His voice was harsh. "Don't move. I have to think. Dear Lord, how can I *think*."

She moved again, instinctively tightening around him.

He was lost.

He groaned deep in his throat and began to thrust. Plunge. His breath came so hoarsely, it was like a sob.

His hands moved around to cup her bottom, and he lifted her, moved her, took her. It was as if he were possessed and in turn had to possess her.

"Sabin. . . ." Mallory could see his face in the blue-lit darkness, and what she saw there both frightened and entranced her. He was absorbing her again, pulling her into himself, making her entirely his own. She felt a sudden flurry of panic. "No."

"It's too late." The words were grated between his teeth, each one hard with pain. "You . . . belong to me. It has to happen."

Her teeth bit into her lower lip as the tension rose to unbearable heights. It had to break.

But it didn't.

She arched up against him. "Sabin, make it—"

She cried out as the tension exploded in searing brilliance.

"That's right, love," Sabin's voice was low, exultant. "Now, just a little more." Several fierce thrusts and then he suddenly froze, throwing back his head, his strong throat arching as a shudder tore through him. He collapsed against her, his big body shaking.

After a moment he looked down at her, his breath coming in gasps. "My God, it tore me apart. I thought I—" He broke off, his expression clouding with concern. "Are you all right?"

"I don't know." She wasn't sure of anything. Sabin still held her, enthralled both physically and emotionally, but tendrils of painful reason were beginning to flow. The television flickered blankly above them, casting its blue light over the shadowy room.

She gazed at it in dumb fascination as Sabin's words returned to haunt her.

He moved off her and stood up. "We have to talk." He picked up his navy blue shirt and draped it around her, thrusting her arms through the sleeves. The shirt smelled of soap and spice, she noticed vaguely. He buttoned the top button, got up again and moved across the room to turn on the desk lamp. He turned to look at her, his expression grim. "We need to get a few things straight. One thing in partic—" He broke off as he saw her face. "What's wrong? Stop staring at that damn screen and look at me."

She couldn't look at him. She couldn't look at anything but the flickering blue light. Sabin Wyatt was sitting there naked beside her. She had let him make love to her in the most intimate way possible between a man and woman. No, not love. It had been lust. She felt the muscles of her stomach twist in rejection at the thought. "It was all true, wasn't it?" she whispered. "About Ben, the tapes. All of it. It was . . . real."

"Of course, it's true." He shut off the television set. "Mallory, I don't know what the hell's happening."

The blankness of the screen released her. She dragged her gaze away and struggled to sit up. "I have to . . . I can't stay here." Waves of darkness began to wash over her as she stood up and stumbled toward the door. "Real . . . Mistake. I can't stay . . ."

"Mallory!"

Why couldn't she make her legs work properly? She felt as if she were wading through mud.

She reached for the knob of the door but it wasn't there.

Nothing was there.
Only blackness.

Sabin looked tired.

At first, Mallory thought she must be mistaken. Since the moment she had first seen him, she had been conscious of his overwhelming vitality dominating everything and everyone around him. Yet now deep grooves lined either side of his mouth, and he was staring at the headboard with a blind weariness that was unmistakable. "You're tired. You . . . should go to . . . bed."

His gaze shifted quickly to her face, and he tensed. "That's a weird thing for you to say. The least I expected was 'Go to hell, Sabin.' "

"Give me time. I just woke up. I'll get there."

"I don't give a damn if you flay me alive. I'm just glad you're finally awake. You scared the hell out of me."

"Did I?" She sat up in bed and lifted her fingers to rub her temple. "Lord, I have a headache."

"You're lucky you don't have more than that." Sabin picked up the brown pill vial from the bedside table. "Didn't anyone ever tell you not to mix pills and booze?"

"I didn't mean to do it. I didn't think . . . It was only a few swallows."

"Enough to do the damage." Sabin put the vial back on the table. "Your Dr. Blairen was mad as hell."

Her gaze flew to his face. "You called him?"

"What did you expect me to do? I carried you back here and found the pills. For all I knew, you might be in a coma."

"You shouldn't have bothered him." She moistened her lips with her tongue. "I was just tired."

"Exhaustion, anemia, severe nervous tension," Sabin enumerated. "In short, within a hair's breadth of a nervous breakdown."

"I'll have to have a talk with the good doctor." She made a face. "There's such a thing as patient confidentiality. Besides, the man worries too much. I'm fine."

"Are you?" Sabin's gaze raked her face. "Is that why you look as delicate as a willow leaf? Is that why you slept for twenty-four hours?"

"That long?" She glanced away from him. "Jet lag." Her slim fingers clenched the sheet nervously. "And a few other shocks to my system."

"I had a few shocks too." He paused. "For instance, your virginity. What the hell—"

"I'd rather not talk about that right now," she interrupted quickly. "I think I'm hungry."

His gaze narrowed on her face. "We're going to talk soon, Mallory." He stood up and moved toward the door. "But right now you do need food more than I need answers. I'll send Nilar in with a tray." He paused at the door to look back at her, and for the first time a smile that held no bitterness softened his harsh features. "I'm glad as hell you've come back to me. Don't you ever do that again."

Then, before she could reply, he was gone.

The room appeared to lose color and vitality, yet Mallory welcomed that loss. She had to think, and she couldn't do it with him sitting there looking at her. Now the tension gripping her eased a little. In her weakened state she was better off without any confrontations with Sabin Wyatt. His effect on her was as unsettling now as it had been in the library when—

She blocked the thought, but it was too late to halt the tingle of heat and anger at the memory of what Sabin had done to her. She could accept the anger as her right, but she mustn't remember her response.

So what was the next move? Did she go to Sabin and rant and rave as he obviously expected? She didn't have the strength to set off the fireworks she would like to light under him, and she had never found anger as successful as reason when confronting anyone of intelligence. No, it was better to submerge the anger and maintain control of the situation.

Control? Her lips twisted as she lay back down on the pillows. She hadn't done too well at maintaining control since she had walked in the front door at Kandrahan. Okay, face it, she told herself. She had made a mistake, but it was no great tragedy. What had happened had been a combination of cause and effect that would never occur again. Shock, exhaustion, pills, the liquor, and Sabin's sexual charisma at full power.

But she was fully herself now and should be able to handle both Sabin and the situation.

Three

Mallory finished the meal Nilar brought her, slept, ate once more, and went back to sleep. It was three o'clock in the afternoon when she awoke again and, for the first time in weeks, she felt fully rested, even energetic.

Two hours later she had showered, shampooed and dried her hair, put on a trim dark blue dress, and set out to find Sabin. She found him sitting at the big mahogany desk in the library carefully studying a document on the paper-strewn blotter. He looked up when she opened the door, and she could feel the sudden tension that gripped him.

"Well, hello." He smiled crookedly as his gaze went to the businesslike dress. "Is that supposed to deter all my lustful tendencies?"

She carefully avoided glancing at the huge television screen dominating the far wall as she closed the door and came toward him. "I like this dress."

"I didn't say I didn't like it. It's just the kind of thing my personnel offices recommend for our secretaries. Definitely no nonsense." He leaned back in his chair, his gaze appraising. "You look better."

"I am better." She braced herself. "And I'd like to leave now, please."

He stiffened. "Really? You've hardly paid your debt with a one-night stand." He paused. "Though I suppose you might consider giving me your virgin—"

"Oh, for God's sake, you're not going to start all that again?" she asked, exasperated. "Virginity in this day and time is only an inconvenience not a pearl without price." She met his gaze directly. "Look, what happened last night was a mistake. If I didn't believe that, I'd be even angrier than I am now. You behaved like an oversexed Neanderthal, and part of me wants to pick up that marble paperweight and brain you with it."

"And the other part of you?"

His smile was blatantly sensual, as sensual as when he had smiled at her last night when he had moved— She quickly looked away from him and down at the marble paperweight. "You're reputed to be an intelligent man. You must have realized by now that the situation wasn't what you thought it was."

"Unless Ben enjoyed you in, shall we say, more 'exotic' ways, I'd say that was abundantly clear." His gaze searched her face. "You didn't know I had the tapes, did you?"

The color rose to her face. "No, and I'd like them back. I burned the originals after Ben's death."

"Mine are copies?"

She nodded. "Look, do we have to talk about this? It's very hard for me."

A faint smile tugged at his lips. "It's been very hard for me too. I think I deserve an explanation."

She caught the double entendre, and a flood of heat surged through her. She avoided his gaze as she dropped down onto the visitor's chair beside the desk. "All right, let's get it over with. What do you want to know?"

"Shall we start with the tapes?"

She looked down at her hands folded on her lap. "Ben was impotent."

Sabin's eyes widened. "The hell he was. And you married him?"

"I didn't know. We didn't . . . He swept me off my feet. We were married a week after we met." She shook her head ruefully. "It wasn't at all like me. I'm usually very practical and cautious. I suppose he caught me at just the right time. I'd been working like a demon to get somewhere careerwise since I was sixteen, and suddenly Ben appeared. He was good-looking, brimming with *joie de vivre* and little boy charm. He opened new doors for me." She smiled sadly. "I fell in love with him."

A distinct edge sharpened Sabin's voice. "I have no desire to hear how irresistible you found him."

"Anyway, Ben was impotent. I wanted to make our marriage work, so I arranged for both of us to go to a therapy clinic." She looked straight ahead. "They said his problem was mental not physical and suggested I do whatever was necessary to—Ben said making and watching the tapes would help."

"I can imagine." Sabin's tone was dry. "They'd arouse a eunuch. What about the ermine coat and the jewelry?"

"Ben said he rented them. I only wore them for the films. I don't know what he did with them afterward." She lifted her gaze to meet his. "The films didn't work. I didn't find out until a few weeks before he died why he didn't find me desirable."

"He was an idiot?"

"Ben was gay. His lover came to see me and asked me to release Ben from our marriage."

Sabin hid his shock.

"Did you tell the police about him?"

She shook her head. "I felt sorry for him. He was a sweet, gentle man, and I think he really loved Ben. He could never have hurt anyone. Why should I involve him?"

"Some people might say it would have helped to take off some of the flack you were getting." He studied her troubled expression for a moment. "You don't understand that viewpoint. Interesting."

"I could handle the flack." She shrugged. "You grow up fast and tough when you're on your own."

"Tough?" He shook his head. "No way."

"I suppose you have a right to think I don't have much backbone based on the way I caved in when—"

"I didn't say I didn't think you had courage. I just said you're about as tough as a day-old kitten." A smile suddenly lit his face. "And I'm happy as a clam about it."

She looked at him startled. "Why?"

"Because I *am* tough and that gives me one hell of an advantage." He stood up and came around the desk toward her.

She instinctively stiffened and took a step back.

He stopped and shook his head. "I'm not stupid enough to approach you now. I made a mistake, and I know I have to make that up to you. Besides, the mark of a good businessman is to analyze the ebb and flow of the marketplace and adjust accordingly."

He reached out one finger and touched her cheek. "And I'm a very good businessman, Mallory."

She could feel her cheek burn beneath the pad of his finger.

She had a sudden vivid picture of herself lying naked on that leather chaise lounge across the room with Sabin looming over her, all muscular power and primitive need.

His smile faded. "Now I wonder what you're thinking about? Perhaps we're having less ebb and more flow after all."

"No." She swallowed and took another step back. "I . . . don't know how my voice came to be on the end of that tape. I didn't say those words."

"Professionals can splice tapes so that the flow between words is seamless. The breaks become indistinguishable. Ben probably thought that was a stroke of genius." He shrugged. "He wasn't far wrong."

"When can I leave here?"

"Are we back to that?"

"Yes." She moistened her lips with her tongue. "I've been thinking about this feeling you had for me, and I've decided it was composed of both annoyance because you thought I'd cheated you and a desire for the unattainable. Now that you know I had nothing to do with Ben bilking you out of that money, one of those reasons should be nullified." She paused. "And you've already had me so I'm no longer unattainable."

"So that should take care of the whole kit and caboodle?" Sabin lifted his brow. "Are you always this analytical?"

She nodded. "It makes life simpler if you try to understand why people act and react the way they do."

"I see." He leaned back against the desk and crossed his arms over his chest. "And I'm supposed to react to your clarification of my unreasonable attitude by letting you go?"

"I hope you will."

He shook his head. "How can I do that, when you just blew it?"

She looked at him in bewilderment.

"You're trying to run away." His eyes twinkled. "That automatically makes you unattainable again."

Her bewilderment turned to surprise. "You're different today."

"I don't go around all the time brooding like Heathcliff and kidnapping nubile young maidens to ravish."

"Only half the time?"

"Scarcely a quarter." He leered melodramatically. "I conserve all my energy so that when I do, I can give it my full attention."

She found herself laughing. "You're joking, right? You realize how foolish this all is?"

"All obsessions are sublimely foolish," he agreed. "That's why they have to be taken seriously." He straightened away from the desk. "Dinner should be ready by now. Would you like a drink first?"

She shook her head. "I'm still taking the pills."

He frowned. "I don't like prescription drugs. They're like guerrillas who sneak up and slice your throat before you even know they're a threat."

"Dr. Blairen said I needed them for a while longer."

"Maybe. We'll talk about it later. Are you hungry?"

"Not really. It seems I've done nothing but eat and sleep for the last two days."

"You needed it." His hand cupped her elbow as he

propelled her toward the door. "You could use at least another ten pounds."

"I'll photograph better at this weight. Everything has an up side."

"Does it?" He opened the door. "You sound like Pollyanna."

She chuckled. "What's wrong with that? Lord, how I hate gloomy, cynical people who won't admit there are still beautiful things in the world." Her smile faded as she looked at him earnestly. "It's going to be all right, isn't it? You're going to be sensible about this?"

"It's going to be fine." He urged her forward into the corridor. "And we'll discuss your departure after dinner."

She smiled, relieved. "I knew you'd be reasonable once the misunderstanding was straightened out."

"Oh, yes, I'm known for being very pragmatic and sensible. I'm not at all like Ben." His lips twisted. "No one in their wildest dreams could call me either charming or irresistible."

"It depends on how the term is used. I have an idea you could definitely be called an irresistible force."

"But you're hardly an immovable object." His keen gaze raked her face. "You obviously have a heart made of mush and can be imposed on by all and sundry."

"Not true."

"No? You allowed Ben to manipulate you shamelessly. You let his lover, who would have been a prime murder suspect, slip out of the spotlight scotfree. You're even making excuses for me." He glanced away from her. "My Lord, and you still say you're tough?"

"You don't have to be aggressive to be strong," she said quietly. "Resilience and endurance are just as important in the long run."

"If you take aggressive action you eliminate the need to endure."

"We're not going to agree on this."

"So you refuse to argue?"

"Why should I? Our viewpoints are obviously light years apart. I'd wager we're not compatible on very many subjects."

"Perhaps." He opened the door to the left of the corridor to reveal a formal dining room. "But sometimes incompatibility on minor points doesn't mean a damn thing if you're compatible on the big ones."

Sabin crouching naked between her thighs, his face glazed with pleasure.

The picture flashed through Mallory's mind bringing with it the now familiar breathlessness. She gazed at him warily. "For instance?"

"World hunger. Should we get rid of the nukes? Do we go to the stars or only try to improve life here on earth?" He smiled innocently as he held her chair for her. "Did you think I meant anything else?"

"No." She sat down and took her napkin from the table. "I only wondered."

Sabin sat down across from her. "Well, should we do it?"

"Do what?"

"Go to the stars." He motioned to the white clad servant hovering nearby to begin serving before he turned back to her. "What's your view on the appropriations for NASA?"

By the time the meal ended, Sabin not only knew her viewpoints on all the subjects he'd mentioned but practically every other topic under the sun. He kept a rapid fire of questions and answers going and seemed genuinely absorbed in her replies.

Mallory found their views seldom coincided, but she found Sabin surprisingly tolerant and ready to listen even when he disagreed. Even the arguments became enjoyable; he displayed a rapier sharp wit and a dry sense of humor that made any conversation stimulating to the point of exhilaration.

"We'll have coffee later," he said as he pushed back his chair after they had finished dessert. "Have you ever seen the desert sky at night?"

She shook her head. "I grew up in Chicago."

"Then you have a treat." He pulled back her chair. "Come out into the garden."

She grinned. "And walk down the primrose path?"

"No primroses in Sedikhan. The flora is much more exotic."

He opened the French doors, and she was immediately bombarded by the scent of jasmine and gardenia.

She breathed deeply as she followed him down the landscaped path. "Wonderful."

"Now look up there." He pointed at the velvety black of the night sky studded with glittering stars. "How can you say we should stay earthbound with all that waiting for us?"

"Ethiopia."

"Jupiter."

"Bangladesh."

"Mush. A heart full of pure mush."

She dropped down on a marble bench by a graceful mosaic fountain and looked up at him. He towered above her, the rich dark brown of his hair almost black in the moonlight. "Is that why you brought me out here? To argue about appropriations for NASA?"

"No." He leaned on the rim of the fountain. "I thought I'd better provide you with the most pleasant setting possible when I told you I wasn't letting you go."

She stiffened. "What? But you said after dinner we'd—"

"Discuss your departure," he finished. "And we are. You're not leaving Kandrahan."

"This is ridiculous."

He shook his head. "I know this throws all your neat little analysis out of kilter, but I don't give a damn about getting even with you and Ben. I never did. I just wanted you."

"You've *had* me, dammit."

"I want you again," he said softly. "And again and again. I want you to be my mistress, Mallory."

"Well, you can't have everything you want. I've no desire to be anyone's mistress. All I want to do is get on with my life. It was all a mistake and—"

"What we had in the library was no mistake." A hint of steel entered his tone. "You enjoyed the hell out of it, and I nearly went crazy."

"Sex." Mallory shook her head. "You can't base a relationship on sex."

"It's done all the time." He paused. "Besides, there may be more between us. It's too soon to tell. I thought you were something you're not, and all this has thrown me a curve." He stopped and when he continued his voice held a note of restrained violence. "I need time to sort things out, and I'm not letting you run away while I do it."

"You think I'll just jump into your bed because you want me to?"

"No." His lips tightened. "I know damn well you won't. That's why I'm grabbing my chance. For heaven's sake, I'm not talking rape, Mallory."

She laughed without mirth. "It sounds remarkably like it."

His hands closed on the rim of the fountain. "Look, you're not well enough to work yet."

"I think that's my decision to make."

"Not while you're under contract to me."

"You?"

"Global."

She stood up, her eyes were blazing at him. "You'd keep me from acting?"

"Until you're entirely well."

"Then I'll get another job. I'll wait tables or—"

"Not in Sedikhan. You don't speak the language."

Her hands clenched into fists at her sides. "I'm beginning to become very angry with you, Sabin."

"I don't blame you. I'd be mad as hell."

"Then let me go."

He slowly shook his head. "Not yet. Give me three weeks."

"To convince me how happy I could be as the outlet for your libido?"

He smothered a smile. "What I'm trying to do is turn back the clock to that first night when I saw you at the premiere, before everything got in our way. I'm not going to try to force you to go to bed with me, and I know bribery wouldn't work now." He shrugged. "That only leaves seduction, and seduction takes time. Give me three weeks to convince you that you'd be happy as my mistress. After that, I'll let you leave Kandrahan and go to Marasef to start work on the picture."

"And stay out of my life?"

"No promises. But I'll stay out of your way until the picture is finished. Deal?"

She gazed at him without speaking, her mind a tumult of anger, hope, and fear. She could feel her confidence and control ebb away. He was making deals and trying to run her life to suit himself. "I don't know. I'll have to think about it."

He nodded. "I thought you would. Tell me tomorrow."

"I'll tell you when I know myself." She whirled on her heel and strode toward the palace. "And not before."

"Yes, ma'am."

He was laughing at her.

She glared at him over her shoulder. "And I am *not* mush."

"I'm beginning to think I exaggerated on that score."

"You're damned right you did."

She swept regally into the house and slammed the door.

She had done that quite well, she thought with satisfaction as she hurried down the hall toward her room. Just like Glenn Close in *Dangerous Liaisons*.

She only wished her confidence was genuine instead of bravado. She knew she would have to agree to the terms Sabin had set for her. She needed that role with Global, dammit.

She just wished she hadn't found Sabin so blasted interesting this evening. It was difficult enough fighting that intense sexual charisma, but tonight she had learned he could also be as stimulating mentally as he was physically. She had actually *liked* the man.

Because he had wanted her to like him, she reminded herself. He had deliberately shown her other facets of his personality so that she could see that the role he wanted her to play in his life would be pleasant.

Pleasant? She had been half out of her head when they had made love, and he had still brought her so much pleasure she couldn't bear to think about it without feeling that same heated response.

But sex wasn't enough, just as the tender, maternal affection she had felt for Ben wasn't enough. She had made one mistake that had nearly wrecked her life, and she wasn't about to make another. A career and friends, while not as exciting, were far safer than the kind of relationship Sabin was offering her.

Now all she had to do was maintain her cool, sensible attitude for the next three weeks.

The next morning, Carey Litzke was sitting at the breakfast table with Sabin when Mallory walked into the dining room. He broke off in midsentence and gazed at Mallory warily. "Hi, I suppose you're ready to draw and quarter me?"

"The thought did occur to me. I'm not at all pleased with you." Mallory sat down across from him and spread her napkin on her lap. She avoided looking at Sabin as she reached for her orange juice. "Sabin told me you were in Marasef. What are you doing here?"

"You said you liked him," Sabin said. "As a gracious host, naturally I wish to provide you with congenial companions. I called Carey last night and asked him to come to Kandrahan to amuse you."

Sabin's planned seduction was obviously beginning, Mallory thought. Instead of furs and jewels, she was being given companions to keep her occupied.

Her tone was barbed as she said sweetly to Carey, "Do you always play court jester when you're not laying traps for poor, unwary ladies?"

Carey flinched. "I wasn't happy about it. I was over the moon when Sabin told me it was only a misunderstanding that's been straightened out now."

"Back off, Mallory," Sabin said. "You know you have no intention of blaming Carey for my sins."

"You're right. But I thought he deserved a few minutes of discomfort for following your dictates so slavishly."

"Slavish isn't a term I'd use for Carey," Sabin said dryly. "He's much more likely to lecture than praise me."

"Good. My opinion of your taste is beginning to rise." Mallory set her orange juice down on the table and smiled at Carey. "You have permission to stay, court jester."

Carey grinned. "I warn you I'm no Robin Williams. My amusement value is on a much quieter plane."

"So is mine." A servant set a plate of melon and strawberries before Mallory and glided silently away. "But there won't be time for much play anyway. I intend to make use of you. I need someone to help me rehearse, and you can cue me."

"Rehearse?" Carey shot Sabin a surprised glance. "I thought she—"

"Mallory would like to be prepared in case she wishes to leave Kandrahan and take over the role in *Breakaway*." Sabin's gaze rested on Mallory's face. "But I believe she's wisely decided to take a three-week vacation before she makes that decision. Isn't that correct?"

Mallory met his gaze. "Partially. The choice is already made, but three weeks of rest won't do me any harm."

"No harm at all," he said softly. "Vacations can sometimes be very pleasurable." He stood up. "And now, if you'll excuse me, Carey brought me some work to do from Marasef. I'll go attend to it so I can be free to enjoy your charming company this afternoon."

She glanced down at her plate. "I intend to be working on the script all day."

"No." Sabin's smile failed to hide his iron determination. "I couldn't think of letting you exhaust yourself. You and Carey can work until two this afternoon on the script, but the rest of the day is mine." He turned to Carey. "If she begins to tire, cut it short. I'm holding you responsible." He turned on his heel and strode out of the dining room.

"What an exit line." Carey made a face. "He puts your back up and turns me into an authority figure instead of a playmate. Diplomacy was never one of Sabin's strong points."

She began to eat her melon. "Have you known him for a long time?"

"Thirteen years. We went to Harvard together, and I started to work for him as soon as he assumed control of Wyatt Enterprises after his father died." Carey lifted his coffee cup to his lips. "He's not as hard as he pretends. He hasn't had an easy life, Mallory."

"Ah, yes, the life of a billionaire is fraught with woe."

"I mean it." Carey's expression was grave. "His father was one of those captain-of-industry types who demand everything and give nothing. From the time Sabin was fourteen he was working for Wyatt Enterprises day and night while trying to keep up his schoolwork."

She shook her head doubtfully. "Ben said his step-father was very indulgent."

"With Ben, not Sabin. Sabin was his own son. He had to measure up." Carey met Mallory's gaze across the table. "And he did measure up to impossibly high standards. He's a giant in more than just phys-ical size. The problem with people who are bigger than life is they tend to ask too much from the people around them."

"Ben?"

He shook his head. "Sabin only asked that Ben give him honesty."

And Ben had failed Sabin as he had failed her, Mallory thought with a pang. "But he asks more from you?"

"You're damned right he does. He works me to the point of exhaustion." Carey grinned. "And then he gives me a year's wages as a bonus and a dream vacation at one of those escapes-of-the-rich-and-famous resorts." His smile faded. "But there's never a vacation for Sabin. He's still trying to measure up."

"Why are you telling me this?"

"Because Sabin won't." He paused. "I think you'll be good for him, and sometimes it's easier to under-stand someone's actions if you know how they think."

She did a double take and then smiled. "That's what I told Sabin."

"I knew we were on the same wavelength." He returned her smile. "Uncomplicated. We work hard and enjoy life and the people around us. We climb step by step and don't try to leap tall buildings with a single bound."

She nodded. "But we get very irritated if someone arbitrarily steps in and blocks that climb."

"Oops." He reached out and poured coffee into her cup from the carafe. "Okay. I'll shut up. I suppose it's natural for you to be on the defensive."

"I'd be insane if I wasn't," she said dryly as she picked up the cup and cradled it in her hands. "You may look at me as therapy for your workaholic boss, but I have a few problems of my own."

"Yes, you do." He hesitated. "Did Sabin tell you he had a private investigating team working on clearing up Ben's murder?"

"No."

"They turned up several bits of information that helped to free you, but it also meant you were under surveillance."

"Charming," she said wearily. "I not only had the police tailing me but a horde of private investigators."

"Sabin's contract with Randolph ran out two days ago, but they sent me one final bit of information you should be advised about. It was in the packet of stuff that arrived yesterday."

She looked at him inquiringly.

"The day after you left New York your apartment was broken into and trashed."

Her hands stiffened on the delicate china cup. "A theft?"

"Nothing seems to have been taken. Your landlady told Randolph's man it was vandalism. Mirrors broken, cushions ripped." He paused. "Photographs slashed. She thought it might be some local hoodlums."

A chill iced through Mallory at the thought of

mindless violence reaching across an ocean to touch her, even here in Sedikhan. "What photographs?"

"Some of your publicity photos." He gazed at her, troubled. "That frightens you?"

A telephone ringing in the night and only silence on the end of the line.

"Yes." Her hand was trembling as she lifted the cup to her lips. "Violence always frightens me. I don't understand it."

"Have there been any other instances like this?"

"Not like this." She looked into the black depths of the liquid in her cup. "Phone calls."

"What?"

"Phone calls. Ever since Ben died there have been phone calls. Every night. Sometimes during the day too. I answer the phone and there's silence, and the phone is hung up."

"A practical joker?"

She smiled with an effort. "I didn't find the joke very funny. I was going through a bad time, and I didn't need that kind of war on my nerves. I started to need pills to sleep at night."

"Why didn't you get your number changed?"

"I did. Twice. And I switched to unlisted. I still got the calls."

"I think we should tell Sabin about this."

"No, it's my business. Sabin's already trying to run my life to suit himself. I'm certainly not going to throw any more bits and pieces of it his way."

Carey's jaw set stubbornly. "Sabin should know. If you won't tell him, I believe I'd better."

Mallory's lips tightened. "You set me up once, Carey. I can forgive one betrayal, but I won't a second."

He flinched. "That stung."

"Most people are hurt by their own actions."

He sighed. "Okay. I won't tell Sabin . . . yet. But I'm going to keep Randolph on the job for a bit longer. Just to see if anything else happens."

"Nothing will happen." She smiled brilliantly at him as she pushed back her chair and stood up. "There's a chance the vandalism has nothing to do with the phone calls."

"That's why you immediately connected the two."

"I've been a little paranoid lately." She crooked her finger at him. "Work."

He rose to his feet. "Cuing you won't be work. You should attend one of Sabin's brainstorming sessions, if you want to see work."

"Don't be so sure. Cuing can be monotonous as the devil." She moved toward the door. "I'll get the script. Meet me in the garden in ten minutes."

"Break time."

Mallory turned to see Sabin coming toward them down the garden path. "I can't stop now. I need to go over this scene again."

"The doctor said you need a nap every day. That takes priority."

"Rescue, at last." Carey sighed as he tossed the script on the bench beside him. "And I thought you were a perfectionist, Sabin. She must have made me go over that scene a hundred times."

"Well, take a break, and then go to the library and fax those contracts to Paris."

"You're going to take the bid?"

"Hell, no, not unless they agree to the clauses I inserted." Sabin's hand closed on Mallory's wrist. "As soon as they get the contract, they're going to call and kick up a fuss. But tell them either to put up or no deal."

"What if they want to talk to you?"

"Tell them I can't be disturbed."

Carey looked at him in surprise. "Well, that's a first."

Sabin was pulling Mallory toward the house. "I have a delicate constitution, and I need my rest."

Carey chuckled. "I can see you're fading away."

"I need to go over this scene," Mallory protested. "And I'm not a child to be sent to her room for a nap."

"Who's sending you to your room? You're going to my suite, and I'm going with you." He pulled her down the hall. "I know damn well you probably wouldn't rest if I left you to your own devices." He slanted her a smile. "You're clearly a project that needs close monitoring."

He threw open a door and pulled her into a large bedroom. The furniture was simpler, the colors bolder than in her own suite. Crimson brocade draperies were pulled back from the long windows and matched the coverlet on the king-size bed. "Lie down."

She stared at him warily.

He shut the door and kicked off his loafers. "Lie down," he said again as he crossed the room and pulled the drapes closed. Dark, softly intimate shadows invaded the room. "Take off your shoes and loosen your clothing." He stood there, waiting. "Come on. Do you need me to help you?"

"I don't mean to stay very long. I need to get that scene right."

"There's plenty of time." He watched her until she settled herself on the crimson coverlet before moving to stand over her. "A three-hour nap and I'll let you work two hours before dinner."

"Let?"

"Poor choice of words." He lay down beside her, not touching her, his gaze on her face. "Open mouth, insert foot. You already know what a rough bastard I am." He rested his cheek on his fist. "Go to sleep."

She chuckled suddenly. "You expect me to go to sleep with you lying there staring at me?"

"Why not?"

"Because I feel as if I'm being stalked."

"If I was stalking you, you'd know it. I'm not subtle."

"If you insist on staying here, why don't you go read a book or something?"

"Because I kind of like lying here and looking at you," he said simply.

She felt an odd melting sensation and quickly lowered her lashes to half-veil her eyes.

"When I'm away from you I forget how beautiful you are. It always comes as a fresh shock." He leaned over and gently passed his hand over her lids, closing them. "But it's even better now. I like the way you look with your black hair all silky and mussed on my pillow." His voice, deep, rich and musical, came softly through the darkness. "And I . . . like taking care of you."

A touch of wonder had threaded his tone. "You sound surprised." She yawned. "Haven't you ever—"

"Shh." She could feel his big body shift on the bed as he drew her close.

She went rigid and then relaxed when she realized there was nothing in the least sexual about the embrace. The heaviness of his arms held only comfort and loving tenderness.

"Isn't this nice?" he whispered, his lips brushing her temple. "You're as soft and cuddly as Old Joe."

"Old Joe?"

"When I was a kid, I had a toy giraffe named Old Joe."

She drew closer. "Why old?"

"He had old eyes. They looked like they'd seen the birth of the earth."

"Most kids have teddy bears."

"Old Joe and I understood each other."

Because Sabin had been forced to be old before his time too, she wondered drowsily. Without thinking, she slid her arms around him and burrowed her face in his shoulder. "I had a panda bear. Actually, I still have him. He's packed away with some furniture and books in a warehouse in Chicago."

"Most kids seem to have bears. They're cuter than giraffes."

She nodded. And their eyes weren't old and weary but bright black buttons, suitable for a child's world. "Where's Old Joe now?"

"Lord only knows. Go to sleep."

She was already half-asleep, she realized. "You, too?"

"I'll try later."

"You should find him."

"Who?"

"Old Joe." Her voice was barely audible. "You should hold onto things you care about. You shouldn't have let him go . . ."

She was deeply asleep.

Sabin lay there as the minutes ticked by, his gaze fastened on the drapes across the room. Lord, he hadn't thought of Old Joe in over twenty years. It was hardly any wonder. Old Joe had belonged to a gentler Sabin Wyatt, a child who hadn't known the world was more often dark than bright and had little place for gentleness or affection.

Sabin's gaze shifted thoughtfully to Mallory's face. He knew why she had resurrected the memory of that time. Mallory, too, possessed a certain gentleness, a seeking for the bright side, a hope for the future.

What the hell had he done to himself by bringing her to Kandrahan? What had started as lust was changing into something else entirely. Lord, he was even indulging in maudlin reminiscences about the boy he had been and a dumb toy giraffe that had probably been thrown away twenty years ago. If he had any sense, he would send her to Marasef tomorrow and get back to the world he could control.

She stirred against him, and he looked down quickly, his arms instinctively tightening in protection and possession.

And he knew he wouldn't be sending her to Marasef tomorrow.

Four

It was nearly six o'clock when Mallory opened her eyes. For a moment she stiffened in alarm as her drowsy gaze met Sabin's watchful stare only inches away.

"Hello." His voice was as alert as his stare and he immediately released her and sat up. "You'd better go to your room now and dress for dinner."

"It's not late." She could have bitten her tongue. It sounded as if she were asking him to let her stay. "I mean, we didn't dine until almost eight-thirty last night."

"But it will be seven-thirty from now on." He stood up, came around the bed, and reached out a hand to pull her to her feet. "You need to get to bed earlier."

"Naps every afternoon, early to bed. I feel like an invalid." She brushed a strand of hair back from her face. "You're not my doctor, Sabin."

"No, but if I were, I'd do a hell of a lot better job than that pill-slinging Dr. Blairen. Since you're in my care for the next weeks, I look upon myself as your guardian." He bent and retrieved her sandals from the floor beside the bed and handed them to her. "Your slippers, Cinderella."

She sat down on the bed and slid her foot into the white sandal. "I can't see you in the role of guardian either."

"You'll find I'm very good at it. I've had a lot of practice." He smiled crookedly. "Though not with people. My experience lies with guarding corporations, but I'm sure the principle is the same."

She put on the other sandal and stood up. "I've never been compared to a corporation before."

"Assets, deficits, vulnerabilities, strengths." He shrugged. "Both corporations and people are a mixed bag. You have to protect and nurture and guard against certain things in both of them."

"But you prefer corporations."

"Usually." His expression became guarded. "It's safer."

She quickly masked the twinge of sympathy she felt at his words. He would neither accept nor appreciate pity. She moved toward the door. "I'll see you at dinner. I have to make a phone call to New York. Will you ask Carey to place it for me through the Sedikhan operator?"

"Who are you going to call?"

She turned as she opened the door and shook her head. "Don't worry, I'm not going to phone the FBI or the State Department. Considering my present notoriety I doubt if they'd pay any attention if I shouted 'wolf'." She suddenly grinned as she realized the unintentional play on words. "Though if the shoe fits . . ."

His light eyes twinkled. "Or the fangs?"

Her smile faded. "The telephone call?"

"You didn't answer me."

"I promised James Delage I'd call when I arrived in Sedikhan. He said Gerda would be anxious about me." She made a face. "He warned me not to come here when I called to say good-bye. I suppose I should have listened to him."

"No, you were right. What was there for you in New York if you hadn't come?"

"Possibilities."

"You have that here." He met her gaze. "Infinite possibilities."

She pulled her gaze away. "I don't want to worry James and Gerda more than they are already. I should have called when I first arrived."

"And are you going to cry wolf to the honorable solicitor?"

"Don't be silly. Why should I worry him when I'm half a world away?"

"Very sensible." The tension ebbed from him. "I didn't want to have to muzzle the man. He did a good job with your defense."

"He's been very kind to me. I don't know what I would have done without him when Ben was shot."

"Gratitude's permitted," he said curtly. "But you don't have to go overboard. I don't like to hear about the men who have been 'kind' to you."

"What do you—" She stopped as she understood. "For heaven's sake, James and Gerda have been married for five years. Do you think I'm some kind of femme fatale?"

"Yes." He didn't look at her as he jammed his foot into his loafer. "You're a woman who men go crazy over. At least, that's been my experience. Why should James Delage escape the net?" He didn't give her a chance to answer. "After you're dressed for dinner, go to the library. I'll have Carey meet you there and place the call."

"Thank you." She started to close the door.

"Wait."

He was frowning at her. "I'm . . . sorry. I shouldn't be barking at you. It's my fault."

She was as surprised by the apology as she was by his words. "What's your fault?"

He was silent a moment. "I'm jealous as hell. I know Delage isn't anything to you but it doesn't help much. I'm not very secure. It's not easy to play the bad guy."

"In most cases villain roles are much richer than that of the hero."

His lips twisted wryly. "But not nearly as rewarding."

"True." She stared at him thoughtfully. "You keep surprising me."

"It's my strategy. I intend to keep you off balance until you fall into my arms."

She slowly shook her head. "I don't think it's calculated. You're clever, but I don't believe that cleverness is Machiavellian." She swung the door shut. "I'll see you at dinner."

"You're just in time." Carey held out the phone to Mallory as she walked into the library. "The phone's ringing now. I placed the call to Delage's office. I didn't have his home number on hand."

Mallory grinned as she took the receiver. "I'm surprised those private detectives were so remiss in their duty."

"We weren't interested in your lawyer until Sabin—" He broke off and smiled sheepishly. "Forget it."

"I think I'd better." The phone was ringing, and she half-sat, half-leaned against the edge of the desk. The receiver was picked up by James's secretary Lila, and Mallory was immediately put through when she identified herself.

"For Lord's sake, Mallory, where the hell have you been?" James's voice was harsher than she had ever heard it. "We've been worried sick about you."

"I'm fine. I just had a little problem placing a call. I'm in the middle of the desert."

"On location?"

"Sort of."

"What do you mean 'sort of'? You're either on location or you're not."

"Stop cross-examining me, James. I'm fine, and I'll be going back to Marasef in three weeks. I'll call you again when I'm permanently located."

"Give me your phone number there."

"No number."

"I don't like this, Mallory. I want you to get on a plane and come home immediately."

She was startled by the sharpness of his voice. "I know you and Gerda are concerned, James, but I don't appreciate orders. I'll come back to New York when the picture's finished."

Silence stretched on the other end of the line. "I'm sorry, Mallory." James's tone was gentle. "I was way out of line." He paused. "I didn't want to tell you this, but the day after you left there was a big spread in *The New York Times* about your departure from New York and the film in Sedikhan. It . . . worried me."

Her hand tightened on the receiver. "Why?"

"Gerda went by your apartment to check out your tenant and discovered—"

"That it was trashed?"

"You know about that?"

"It's nothing to worry about. It was probably just some hoodlums."

"Maybe. But the police haven't arrested any of those mobsters Ben owed money to yet." He went on quickly, "Anyway, Gerda and I didn't like the idea of every nut in New York knowing where you could be found. You understand that we only want what's best for you?"

Warmth surged through her. "Yes. And this *is* best for me. Nothing can happen to me here. Don't worry, Sedikhan is actually very civilized."

"And you'll call me as soon as you reach Marasef?"

"The first day. Give my love to Gerda."

"I will." James was silent again. "Take care of yourself."

"Good-bye, James." Mallory hung up the receiver.

"You're frowning." Carey stood up. "I take it Delage wasn't pleased?"

She shook her head. "He was really upset, and he's usually so calm. I feel guilty. I should have called him earlier."

"It's water under the bridge now. You weren't to blame for getting ill." He grinned. "But Sabin will hold me to blame if I don't get you in to dinner and get some vittles in you."

She smiled. "Vittles?"

He took her elbow and propelled her toward the door. "Not a Harvard term. Something about you draws me back to my roots."

"And where are they?"

"The mountains of West Virginia."

"I've never been there."

"You've missed white lightning and granny medicine?"

"To my supreme regret."

"I guess I'll just have to tell you about them."

"Not now, Carey." Sabin stood in the hall a few yards away. His gaze shifted to Mallory. "Did you make your call?"

"Yes."

His grasp was light but firm as he took her arm from Carey, and his face expressed only friendly politeness. "Good, now we can forget New York and concentrate on the pleasures at hand."

"What pleasures?"

He smiled. "You persist in misinterpreting me. I was speaking of dinner, conversation, and Monopoly."

"Monopoly?"

"After dinner. I'm good at it."

"It's a game of luck."

"Then I'm lucky." He slanted a grin at Carey. "Right?"

Carey nodded gloomily. "He always wins."

"Not always." He didn't look at Mallory as he ushered her into the dining room. "But I make sure the percentages are on my side."

The next afternoon and every afternoon thereafter Sabin came for Mallory and took her to his room for a nap. She came to think of those periods of rest as a serene oasis in a scorching journey through a desert of sensuality. At all other times Sabin had no qualms about exerting his sexual charisma. And she was finding it increasingly difficult to resist him, but, strangely, he never tried to seduce her in this place where it would be the most easy to succumb. During those hours he was a simpler, less guarded man. By the time a week had passed, the afternoon hours she spent in bed with Sabin seemed as easy and comfortable as if they had been married for fifteen years.

"You've gained a few pounds." Sabin leaned against the headboard and regarded her critically. "Maybe five." He grinned. "Pretty soon you'll be too fat to photograph well. What will you do then?"

"Lose it." She settled on the bed beside him. "Thanks for calling my attention to it. A two day's fast should take care of it."

His smile vanished. "The hell you'll lose it. I was joking. You were too thin before."

"Not before the camera. Now hush and let me sleep."

"You won't fast."

"We'll see."

"No." She felt the mattress shift as he slid down to lay beside her. "You won't fast. It's got to be—No."

"You brought it up."

"I just wanted to see if I could ruffle your feathers. You're so calm all the time. I didn't think you'd take me seriously."

"My appearance is part of my job. I have to take it seriously." Her gaze narrowed on his face. "Why are you so upset? A two-day fast won't harm me."

"My father's third wife was an anorexic. She died of heart failure brought on by dieting and pills."

Mallory went still. "How terrible. Were you close?"

Sabin shrugged. "I liked her better than the others. She was nice to me, and she didn't have to make the effort. My father never married his wives for their maternal qualities."

"Why did he marry them?"

"Money and sex. Except my mother. He married her to get an heir. He always wanted a dynasty and was disappointed by Margaret, his first wife. He divorced her after three years. My mother proved more fertile." His lips twisted. "Unfortunately, she wasn't as good in bed as the next candidate for his hand, so, after he paid her off for signing over custody of me, she faded away into the sunset."

"Faded away?"

"It seems a suitable term. She married a college professor and apparently lived happily ever after in Ivy League heaven."

"How many women did your father marry?"

"Five. Ben's mother was the last to occupy my father's bed."

"Your father evidently liked variety."

"He was a realist. He knew no relationship lasted forever. When the glow faded, he cut his losses and went on to someone else."

Mallory felt a wrenching pang as she looked at Sabin. "And that's the way you feel, too, isn't it?"

He met her gaze. "It's dangerous to imagine anyone's irreplaceable. People change."

"But that's the challenge," Mallory said. "Growing together, instead of apart. My mother and father would have stayed together for the next fifty years if they hadn't died in that car crash."

"How do you know?" Sabin smiled crookedly. "Maybe if they'd lived, your father would have found some teenager who made him feel young again and your mother some kid who—"

"No! They loved each other." Mallory's eyes were bright with tears. "They would have loved each other forever and ever. I remember how my mother would look when my father walked into the room. It wouldn't have changed no matter how old they grew. It wouldn't have—"

"Shh." Sabin's fingers gently stroked the soft hair at her temple. "I didn't mean to upset you. Maybe your parents were the exception to prove the rule."

"And the rule is that no relationship lasts?" Mallory shook her head. "I can't believe that." She raised herself on one elbow and looked down at him. "But you do. What does last, Sabin?"

"Work. Purpose. Character."

"What about friendship? Carey's been your friend for over thirteen years. Are you going to walk away from him someday because you've changed and he's stayed the same?"

Sabin frowned. "I don't walk away from my friends."

"Then you've just invalidated your argument."

"Friendships are different. It's relationships between men and women that are dangerous." He shook his head. "You can't keep a sloop moored in a rotting pier. Someday it will just pull free and drift away."

"And is affection the rotting pier or the sloop? Either way the metaphor is *wrong*."

"I refuse to argue with you about this," Sabin said quietly. "If I had had any idea it would disturb you, I wouldn't have started the discussion. I should have known you'd argue with me. It's a no-win subject like religion and politics."

"Yes. It's a no-win argument." She closed her eyes so that he wouldn't see just how upset she had become. It was clear Sabin had been damaged from a childhood dominated by a father who traded in wives as if they were cars, and held neither hope nor illusion. That knowledge shouldn't have brought on a feeling of melancholy, a sense of something lost. In two weeks she would go to Marasef, and her time with Sabin would be at an end. She would *not* feel sorry for that child, even though no one had taught him that anything beyond work had lasting value. He was occupying entirely too many of her thoughts these days as it was.

"No fasts."

She opened her eyes. "What?" She had forgotten for the moment how the discussion had started, but it was like Sabin to cling tenaciously to what he wanted, undeterred by anything else in his path.

"I'll see when I get to Marasef."

A frown furrowed his brow. "I don't want to hear—" He broke off and the frown faded. "That's two weeks away. I'll keep my mouth shut, and maybe you'll forget it."

"I don't forget," Mallory said. "Sometimes I wish I did. It would be easier." She closed her eyes again and flowed toward him and into his arms with incredible ease. Outside the room Sabin was a danger, a threat, but here he was safety and strength. "Let's go to sleep, Sabin."

His arms tightened around her, and his lips brushed her forehead. "I'm sorry."

"For what?"

"That I can't believe what you believe."

The Sabin outside this room would have been too armored to say he was sorry, she thought. "There's no reason to be sorry. We've disagreed on many things before," she whispered as she settled her cheek more comfortably on his shoulder. "This is just another one."

"But I think this is more important to you."

His voice was beautiful. She usually loved to lie here with her eyes closed and listen to the deep rich timber, the precision with which he enunciated each word, but she didn't want to hear him speak now. His words were causing a hollow ache within her, stronger than anything she had ever felt before. "I don't want to talk about it. I want to go to sleep."

"All right."

The dusky intimacy of the room enclosed them with its shadowy silence, and they spoke no more.

But for the first time since he had begun bringing her here, neither of them slept.

"I like you in that red silky thing you're wearing today."

"It's a halter top, and it's not red, it's maroon. I never wear red."

"Why not? With your dark hair it would be striking."

She settled closer to him. "It's too showy."

"And you're not an exhibitionist." Sabin's voice was thoughtful. "Actually, you're shy. Those tapes must have been hard for you to make."

"Yes."

"But you made them anyway."

"You don't allow fear to keep you from doing something you believe worthwhile."

"They were beautiful. *You're* beautiful."

She was silent, unconsciously stiffening against him.

"You don't like me to say that. Interesting."

"You have that dissecting note in your voice again. I think it's time for me to go to sleep."

"Not yet. Why don't you like me to tell you how beautiful I think you are?"

"Because I'm more, dammit."

He levered himself up on one elbow, trying to see

her expression in the dimness of the room. "Such vehemence."

"Ever since I was a child whenever someone saw me they'd pat me on the cheek and say, 'Oh, my, what a pretty girl.' Never, what a bright girl or nice girl or talented girl. They only saw what was on the surface. That's all anyone ever sees when they look at me."

"I imagine in your career your looks have been an asset."

"Yes and no." She grimaced ruefully. "James says I have a face as memorable as the Mona Lisa. A face like that opens doors, but how many roles do you think are out there for a Mona Lisa? It's a real world, and the audience wants to identify with real people on the screen. So I have to work harder to make everyone forget my looks and realize I'm approachable."

He chuckled. "I never found myself put off by your face."

"But have you ever thought about me as a person? I'm a good actress. I play the piano badly, and I usually end up by giving more than I can afford to the Humane Society because those pictures they send in their letters hurt me so terribly. I'm fairly literate and intelligent, and I'm loyal to my friends. I'm *more* than what's on the surface, and I hate not being—"

"I believe you."

She stopped, looking up at him in surprise. "You do?"

He nodded. "Absolutely. Evidently when you look in the mirror you don't see what I see."

"What do you see?"

"Character, intelligence, humor, warmth, determination."

"All of that?"

"Don't you know that's what makes you special? Why people turn and look at you on the street? It's not that wonderful bone structure or your eyes or the way you move. It's *you*."

She blinked. "That's quite . . . eloquent."

"I have an idea you need eloquence. I think some of those people who patted your cheek when you were a kid got through to you."

"What do you mean?"

"You try to believe you're more than a pretty face, but you're not really sure."

"No?"

"No." His finger gently traced the line of her left eyebrow. "But I'm sure. When you get old and gray and wrinkled as a prize bulldog, you'll still be as interesting and worth knowing as you are right now."

Warmth rushed through her. "Thank you."

"You're welcome." He lay back down and drew her close again. "Now you can go to sleep."

She lay there thinking about his words and the unexpected sensitivity and understanding he had shown her.

She suddenly giggled.

"What's funny?"

"I just had a vision of the Mona Lisa with the face of a bulldog."

"At least, I said you'd be a prize bulldog."

"Are they less ugly?"

"No, but they have more character."

"Oh, that's all right then."

Three afternoons later Mallory stretched lazily, coming awake slowly, gently as she usually did after her nap. As she sat up, she noticed that the room seemed dimmer than usual. "Lord, what time is it?"

"After eight."

"I was supposed to meet Carey in the garden at seven." She swung her feet to the floor. "I don't know why I've been sleeping so long for the past few days."

"Perhaps because you don't sleep at night." Sabin sat up and leaned back against the headboard, watching her as she stood up and tucked her blouse into her jeans. "I know I haven't had a good night's sleep since you came here."

"I rest very well." But it wasn't true, she didn't sleep. She tossed and turned for the greater part of every night. The only time she had slept soundly during the last week were the afternoons when she lay in Sabin's arms.

"Don't lie to me, Mallory. You forget that I've made a study of your exceptionally lovely physique. I can tell when there's a hair out of place or the faintest shadow beneath your eyes."

She felt the color sting her cheeks. "I told you, I do rest." She turned to face him but he was only a dark silhouette in the dusk-cloaked room.

"Without pills?"

She hesitated. "When I can. I took one last night."

"They're not good for you." He paused. "Come to me."

"What?"

"When you can't sleep, come to me." His voice was rich, reverberating in the darkness with beautiful clarity. "And we'll both sleep better."

She tensed. "Will we?"

"Yes, we've grown used to each other in these last two weeks. I think we need each other."

"All the more reason to break the habit."

"Did it ever occur to you that some habits are good for you? I'm a hell of a lot better than pills. Trust me."

"These are the only times I feel I can trust you."

"Then stretch that trust a little longer. My word is good. If you come to me tonight, I'll treat you exactly as I do every afternoon."

"I don't need you to sleep any more than I do those pills."

"Why did you need those pills to begin with?"

A telephone ringing shrilly in the middle of the night.

"I was going through a rough patch."

"But you're a very strong woman. I wouldn't think you'd stumble into that pit. I wonder . . ." He trailed off as he gazed at her thoughtfully. "It's been bothering me lately that you're always so calm and disciplined."

"Why should it bother you? It's my nature."

"Is it?"

"Yes, and it has nothing to do with my taking those pills."

His lips twisted. "But the pills supposedly keep you serene and better able to face the world. Do you need that help?"

"Are you trying to psychoanalyze me?"

"I'm trying to understand you. Were your parents as placid as you are?"

She laughed with genuine amusement. "My parents were the most volatile, impulsive people you could ever hope to meet. Not at all like me. They were always arguing or making love or—"

"It sounds like you were the outsider. That must have been lonely for you."

"They never meant to make me feel . . . You're misinterpreting what I'm saying. I loved them very much, and they loved me too. Someone had to strike a balance."

"So to strike that balance, you had to be the one in the family who was always in control, the eye in the center of the hurricane. I'll bet you've never acted on impulse in your life." He added softly, "Except when you married Ben."

She didn't like his probing. She felt more vulnerable than when she lay naked before him on that chaise lounge in the library. "Which says a good deal for the virtue of ignoring your impulses. Believe me, my marriage to Ben taught me a number of unpleasant lessons."

"And so you smother your temper and always act reasonably and in complete control."

"Why not? It's the civilized way."

"But is it *your* way? It would be interesting to find out."

"It's my nature," she repeated as she moved toward the door. "I'll see you at dinner."

His voice followed her. "I hope you're right about the pills, but I think you've been on them too long to cut off easily. Wash them down the drain and then come to me."

Mallory stared with revulsion at the brown vial on the night table. She disliked the pills as much as Sabin did, and she knew she shouldn't have given in and taken one last night. But it was over. She wouldn't take the blasted things tonight or ever again.

Three hours later she was still awake staring into the darkness.

Come to me.

Sabin's rich voice coming from the darkness. Rest. Serenity. Strength.

She turned on her side and tried to shut out the memory that held out a more potent temptation than the brown vial on the nightstand.

Come to me.

"Did you take the pills?"

"No."

"But you didn't sleep either." Sabin's index finger traced the shadows beneath her eyes. "You should have—"

"I hate people who tell me what I should do," she interrupted as she lay down on the bed and went into his arms. She wearily closed her eyes. Home. Safety. She could sleep now. Sabin would keep her safe.

His voice came through the darkness as beautiful and strong as his arms holding her secure. "You should have come to me."

"Did you take the pills?"

"I told you I don't take them any longer."

"Then throw them away."

"That would be foolish. I might need—"

She stopped as she realized the word she had used.

Dependency.

"Yes," he said softly. "The guerrilla sneaking up to slash your throat. Throw them away, Mallory."

"Be quiet, Sabin." Her arms slid around him. It was strange how afraid she had been of him in the beginning. Now she looked forward to these hours in his arms with a sort of dark, sweet hunger. She would catch herself looking at the clock when she was rehearsing with Carey.

Only three hours and she could come to Sabin.

Only two hours and Sabin would hold her and she could rest.

He would stroke her hair and when she woke the world would be fresh and new.

Only one hour and he would draw the curtains and talk to her, his voice soft as velvet and bright as thunder in the dimness.

He bent forward, his words only a breath of sound in her ear. "Come to me."

The pill was small and yellow in the palm of her hand. It looked as harmless as an M&M candy.

She closed her eyes.

It wasn't harmless. It was a guerrilla with a machete.

Well, she wouldn't let her throat be cut.

Her eyes opened, she threw the pill into the sink and washed it down the drain with the glass of water she had poured to ease it down her throat.

Then she took the brown vial and emptied it into the toilet and flushed down the pills.

Gone.

Sudden panic bolted through her. She was free, but it didn't feel like freedom. It felt . . . frightening.

She turned and ran from her suite and down the long corridor. A moment later she threw open the door of Sabin's suite.

The bedroom was dark but only a little darker than the artificial dusk to which she had become accustomed.

"It's about time. I've been waiting for you." His voice, coming from the direction of the big bed across the room, sounded wide awake. The light from the hall behind her poured into the room, and she could dimly discern Sabin leaning against the headboard as she had seen him so many times before.

She stood in the doorway, her breasts lifting and falling with her quickened breathing. "I threw the pills away."

"Good."

"I'm scared."

"Bad." He moved over and patted the bed. "Come home."

Home.

She flew across the room.

He held back the covers, and she dove beneath them and into his arms.

She inhaled sharply. He was naked. "You're not dressed."

He chuckled. "What did you expect? I don't sleep in my clothes." His hand began to smooth her hair. "It's only a minor difference."

His body pressed against her own, warm and strong, different yet blessedly the same. She began to relax. "I shouldn't be here."

He didn't answer. He began to stroke her hair.

"Why have you been so kind to me? When you forced me to stay here, I expected something else entirely."

"Why shouldn't I be kind to you when it pleases me as much as it does you?"

"Will you talk to me? I like to hear your voice."

"What do you want me to say?"

A phrase suddenly popped into her mind that frightened her as much as the little yellow pill.

She quickly banished the thought. "Anything."

"Shall I tell you about my new deal with those French vintners? That should put you to sleep in record time."

"I don't care." She breathed deeply. She loved the way he smelled of soap and spicy cologne. His warmth enveloped her, holding off the darkness. "Whatever you like."

"Whatever I like?" His voice was suddenly thick. "I think not." He paused. "I'll tell you about my first semester at Harvard. That should amuse you. It was the year I did everything wrong."

"You?"

"I know it's hard to believe, but even I went through a cocoon stage before I evolved into the perfect being I am now."

She chuckled and drew closer.

It was going to be all right. She had been foolish to worry. She should have come to him sooner.

Five

The touch of Sabin's lips on her closed lids was butterfly-soft, warm as morning sunshine. "Wake up." The words were spoken in a voice as soft as his lips.

She slowly opened her eyes to see him smiling down at her. He was leaning over her, his hands bracing his weight. The sheet had fallen away to reveal the chestnut hair thatching his chest.

"What big eyes you have. Aren't you going to wish me good morning?"

A melting started somewhere in her stomach and spread swiftly through her body. She had a sudden desire to reach out and run her fingers over his chest, feel that virile mass of hair beneath her palms. Incredibly, her breasts began to swell, pushing at the satin confines of her nightgown, the nipples hardening, readying.

The hot color scorched her cheeks as his gaze moved down, lingering on that explicit physical betrayal.

"Never mind." His smile faded and his expression became blatantly sensual. "I'd rather have this kind of salutation any day."

The air between them was so charged she had trouble breathing. "I . . . want to get up now."

"That's not what you want," he said thickly, his gaze on her breasts. With an obvious effort he shifted his glance to her face. "I could make love to you now. It wouldn't take much to push you over the edge."

Her heart leapt and then began to pound erratically. He smelled of cologne and clean soap. His body was hard, powerful above her, and her own body felt soft and pliant, more consciously feminine than she had ever known it to be. She gazed up at him as if mesmerized.

He leaned slowly toward her, and she held her breath, her body tensing in anticipation. The rough mat of his chest hair brushed against her breasts. Even through the satin material of the gown, she could feel his male fur caressing her nipples. The sensation was unbearably erotic.

She inhaled sharply, her fingers digging into the sheet covering the mattress.

Sabin moved his torso back and forth slowly, lazily, his eyes narrowed to watch her expression.

"But I'm not going to do it. Not today." His lips brushed her forehead before he threw back the covers and got out of bed. "A cold shower for me. You just lay there and relax."

Relax? She watched him move across the room. Every muscle of his nude body spoke of coiled tension and arousal, yet it was clear he had no intention of satisfying that arousal. "I don't understand you."

He paused in the doorway to glance ruefully down at his lower body. "I can see how you'd get mixed signals." His gaze lifted to her face. "I'm not interested in quickies. Three hours after I set eyes on you, I was making love to you on that damn chaise lounge in the library. I have to show you that we can have more together." His gaze moved slowly over her. "Do you think every time I lay beside you on that bed I don't remember how it felt to be inside you? But I had to get to know the way you thought as well as what turned you on. We started our relationship at the wrong end, and now we have to work backwards." He turned on his heel and disappeared into the bathroom.

Mallory gazed at the closed door, only subliminally conscious of the sound of the spray of the shower. Panic rose, tightening her chest. What the devil had she gotten herself into? She knew how dangerous it was to act impetuously, and yet she had let Sabin lead her down the path of least resistance because he had made himself appear to be no threat. She had taken the comfort and solace he had offered and let him lull her into a state of contentment that bordered on an addiction as dangerous as those blasted pills.

Perhaps more dangerous.

Sabin's restraint just now bespoke a steely determination far more threatening than the uncontrolled desire he'd shown her the night she had arrived at Kandrahan. She had moved toward him, haltingly at first, then trustingly, and last night had been the final step to place herself unconditionally in his power.

It had to stop.

Mallory threw the sheets aside and jumped out of bed and grabbed Sabin's robe from the chair.

A moment later the door slammed behind her, and she was walking quickly, almost running, down the hall toward her own suite.

Sabin knocked perfunctorily on the door of Mallory's suite but didn't wait for an answer before walking into the room. His gaze went to the open suitcase on the bed. "Nilar said you were packing. May I ask what this is all about?"

"I want to go to Marasef." Mallory didn't look at him as she opened the bureau drawer, took out a pile of silken lingerie, and crossed the room toward the suitcase on the bed. "Right away."

"I still have two days left of my three weeks."

She shook her head. "I don't want to stay here any longer."

He closed the door and leaned back against it. "Why not?"

"I think you know. I've been an idiot." She tossed the lingerie into the suitcase. "I believe you must have hypnotized me or something. I thought everything was going to be . . ." She trailed off and shrugged helplessly. "I'm getting in too deep. This isn't what I want. Another week of this and I'll probably be content to do whatever you want me to do."

He smiled. "Would that be so bad? You're not being mistreated."

"Yes, it would be bad." She crossed to the bureau and scooped up another armload of clothes. "I'm not like you. A relationship has to have substance for me to—We're not alike." She walked across the room and dropped the clothes into the suitcase. "It's best that I go,"

"The hell it is."

She looked at him for the first time since he had entered the room, and a ripple of shock ran through her. Sabin's mouth was drawn in a thin line, and his light eyes blazed hard and bright. She moistened her lips with her tongue. "You promised you'd let me go in three weeks."

"And I'll keep my promise." Sabin moved across the room and slammed the suitcase shut and knocked it off the bed. "In two days. Dammit, I've behaved like a blasted eunuch for the past few weeks. I'm not letting you panic and run out on me just because you suddenly realized that you want me as much as I want you."

"I don't want—" She stopped as she remembered the wave of raw desire that had swept over her only a few hours ago. "There's chemistry between us, but that's not enough for me. A relationship has to mean something besides sex."

"It *does* mean something," he said harshly. "It means—" He broke off and turned away. "I don't know what it means yet, but you're not leaving. In two days I'll drive you to Marasef myself, but I will have those two days, dammit."

The door slammed behind him.

"You look as uptight as Sabin." Carey's gaze searched Mallory's face as she came down the garden path toward him. "Trouble in paradise?"

"Kandrahan isn't paradise." Mallory plopped down beside him on the bench in the enclosed arbor. "And there's certainly nothing celestial about Sabin."

"No, but he's not Mephistopheles either. He's just a man." He smiled gently. "I don't think he knows what to do about you, and that frustrates the hell out of him."

"I'll tell you what he can do. He can let me go."

"He had to let too many people go when he was a kid. He finds it hard to give up what he wants now."

"Until he's ready to boot them out of his life."

"What do you want me to say?" Carey asked. "I won't lie to you and tell you Sabin believes in long-term relationships. I don't remember any affair he's had lasting over three months."

Pain surged through her, as inexplicable as it was intense. How stupid to react like this when she had no desire to throw herself into the lion's den of another no-win relationship. "No, I don't want you to lie to me," she said dully. "I just don't want to be another statistic in Sabin's past date column. I think I have more to give a man than he obviously wants from me." She turned to face him. "Will you help me leave here today?"

He shook his head. "Sabin's my friend as well as my employer, Mallory. I won't jeopardize our relationship." His hand covered hers on the bench. "He's as confused as you are. He's never felt like this about a woman before, and he doesn't like it one bit. Give him a chance."

"I can't give him a chance." She jumped to her feet and picked up the script. "We're through rehearsing. I know this role backwards and forwards."

"That's for sure. So do I. What shall we do instead?"

"*We'll* do nothing. Your services as court jester are officially at an end, Carey." She turned on her heel. "I'm going for a little walk in the desert."

He frowned. "Walk in the desert? Why not stay in the garden. You can't walk in this heat."

"Believe me, the temperature isn't what's making me hot under the collar. I'm going to Marasef."

His eyes widened in alarm. "You can't do that."

"The hell I can't. I'm tired of being sweet, placid Mallory. It's time I acted, instead of reacted."

"Don't do anything foolish. I don't—Lord, I wish I could help you."

"I wish you could too. But since you can't, I'll just have to help myself." She walked away from him down the path.

"Where the hell do you think you're going?" Sabin rode the brake, and the Jeep coasted beside her.

She didn't look at him as she trudged down the road, her gaze on the dunes shimmering on the horizon. "What does it look like? I'm going to Marasef. Go back to the house, Sabin."

"Not until you go with me. For Lord's sake, I couldn't believe it when Carey told me you'd just calmly decided to leave Kandrahan. It's almost a hundred degrees out here." He jammed on the brake and jumped out of the Jeep. "Do you want to undo all the progress you've made in the past three weeks?"

She kept on walking. "I'm wearing a hat and desert boots." She gestured to the two straps crisscrossing her breasts. "And carrying two canteens. The walk won't hurt me."

"How do you know?" He gripped her shoulders and spun her around to face him, his eyes squinting against the white hot glare of the sunlight as he looked down at her. "And how are you supposed to find your way to Marasef?"

"Just follow the yellow brick road," she said flippantly.

"This isn't Oz. You could die out here."

"I won't die, and I *will* go to Marasef." She gazed directly into his eyes. "Count on it. Dammit, I don't want to be here!"

His gaze narrowed on her face. "You're upset."

"How perceptive of you. Don't be an idiot. Of course, I'm upset," she said in exasperation. "Upset, helpless, and fed up. How do you expect me to feel?"

"I don't know." His lips twisted. "I've been too busy trying to make some sense out of how I feel to try to second-guess you." His brow furrowed in a frown. "Okay. Let's deal."

She looked at him warily.

"It's almost four o'clock now. Come back and spend the rest of the day and evening with me, and I'll take you to Marasef tomorrow morning." He saw her wary expression and shook his head. "I don't mean in bed unless you decide you want to be there." He paused. "Though it's only fair to warn you, I'm going to do my damnedest to persuade you to let me make love to you."

She hesitated.

"Persuade, not force," he said softly. "Only half a day. Then 'Hi ho, hi ho, it's off to Marasef we go.'"

"Snow White and the Seven Dwarfs," she said absently, but her gaze was uncertain.

"And I promise not to tempt you with a poison apple."

"I was thinking more on the lines of the apple of knowledge the serpent offered Eve in the Garden of Eden." A sudden smile lit her face. "There's definitely a comparison there."

"Not really." His hands kneaded her shoulders,

and she was reminded of those many hours in his bed when his big hands had soothed and petted her. "You've already tasted the apple and found it to your liking."

"I have no intention of tasting it again."

"Intentions sometimes alter with circumstances. Deal?"

She was silent a moment. His smile was as gentle as the ones he had given her each afternoon when she had nestled in his arms, and yet he was giving her few promises this time. She should refuse this bargain. If she pushed a little more, she might still achieve the total victory she had sought when she left Kandrahan. Yet following that discreet path filled her with an odd reluctance. She had shared too much with Sabin Wyatt in the last weeks to want to end their relationship with anger. In many ways she respected and admired him more than any man she had ever known. Perhaps if she gave them both the opportunity, there might be some way they could forge a tentative friendship.

And she desperately wanted that chance, she suddenly realized. "Deal."

A brilliant smile lit his face. "Great. Let's get you back to Kandrahan and out of this sun." He took her elbow and propelled her toward the Jeep. "You know, you're turning out to be a very surprising lady. I thought I could gauge your reactions, but I never imagined you'd give in to impulse and pull a crazy stunt like this."

A small smile tugged at her lips. "Didn't you?"

He shook his head as he lifted her into the passenger seat of the Jeep. "I didn't think you'd let all that calm, cool reasoning be blown away by emotion."

"You never know about people, do you?"

"Let me take those canteens for you. The straps must be cutting into your shoulders. You look like a guerrilla fighter wearing a banderole of bullets."

"If you like." She pulled the straps of the two canteens over her head and handed the containers to him. "Though they're not at all heavy."

"They have to be. They're two quart—" He broke off as he weighed the canteens in his hands. "Good Lord, they're—"

"Empty." She nodded serenely. "I didn't see any sense in burdening myself too heavily when I might have to walk awhile. I wasn't sure when Carey would get around to telling you I was leaving."

He gazed at her blankly. "A setup."

"Why should I be the only one to be manipulated?" She smiled. "You see, I've been studying you for the last few weeks, too, Sabin. You're not as hard as you think you are. I knew you wouldn't let me run the risk of hurting myself even if it meant giving up what you wanted."

"Well, I'll be damned."

"I hope not. Though I admit I was fervently wishing that state on you this morning."

He threw back his head and laughed. "I love it." A smile lingered on his lips as he strode around the Jeep and jumped into the driver's seat. He gave her a sidewise glance that held amusement, respect, and challenge. "It's your game, Mallory, but one of these days you're going to forget all about reason and act purely on emotion."

"Perhaps." Her own smile faded as she watched him start and reverse the Jeep. By compromising and returning to Kandrahan she was very much afraid, she was already acting purely on an emotional level. The burst of contentment and anticipation exploding within her as she thought about this last night was too intense to mistake.

"Did you wear that for me?" Sabin's gaze went over Mallory slowly, lingering on her bare shoulders framed by the violet chiffon gown.

"It's only polite to try to please one's host." Mallory avoided his stare as she came into the salon. "This is my last night here, and you said you liked violet."

"I do." He held out her glass of white wine. "Thank you."

"Where's Carey this evening?" Mallory carefully avoided looking at Sabin as she sipped her wine.

"I told him to make himself scarce." One corner of Sabin's lips lifted in a lopsided smile. "In my usual diplomatic fashion."

"I hope you weren't rude to him."

"Carey's used to me. I assure you he's not sulking in his room. He knows this may be my last chance to be alone with you at Kandrahan."

She felt the same poignant pang of sadness she had experienced this afternoon. "It will be strange leaving here. These weeks have been very restful."

He chuckled. "Do you know how weird that sounds? I tricked you into coming here, took your virginity, and forced you into staying another three weeks. You should be seething with resentment."

"I'm not good at resentment or anger," she said lightly. "I believe it's better to try to understand than to beat my fists bloody fighting."

His smile faded. "I know. You have the sweetest nature of any man, woman, or child I've ever encountered."

She was embarrassed. "Nonsense."

He shook his head. "I couldn't believe it either." He looked down at the wine in his glass. "I didn't want to believe it. It disturbs me."

"Why?"

He shrugged. "Because I suppose your vulnerability roused any tatters of chivalry that remained in me."

"I think you may be more chivalrous than you think," she said quietly. "You've been very kind to me since that first night."

"Ah, but that's because I wanted to chain you to me in all the ways there are." He lifted his glass to his lips. "You should know by now that kindness isn't one of my more salient qualities."

And he had succeeded in chaining her, she realized suddenly. Why else had she been torn between wanting her freedom and maintaining some kind of bond with Sabin. "You're not as calculated as you pretend." She put her glass on the table beside her. "Isn't it time to go in to dinner?"

"Not yet." He set his own glass down and grasped her wrist. "I want you to come to the library with me."

She stiffened. "Why?"

He was pulling her toward the door. "Are you getting a flash of déjà vu? Don't worry. I'm not stupid enough to try a repeat performance of that first night." He propelled her down the hall and threw open the door of the library. A small fire burned in the fireplace, casting a cozy glow over the book-lined room. Sabin didn't bother to turn on the lights as he released her wrist and closed the door. "They're on the mantle."

"What?"

He strode across the room toward the fireplace. "Come on. Let's get it over with."

She frowned in puzzlement as she slowly followed him across the room.

He turned and gestured to the mantle as she reached the hearth. "Burn them."

Her gaze turned to the six black boxes stacked neatly on the mantle. She went still. "The tapes?"

He nodded. "I could have done it, but I thought you'd rather do it yourself. You'll feel better if you know they're destroyed."

"Yes." She moved a step closer to stand before the fire, feeling the caress of heat through the sheer chiffon of her gown. "I told you that you were kinder than you believe. Why else would you do this for me?"

"I don't need them any longer. They'd only disappoint me." He met her gaze. "They were only erotic dreams. Dreams are as dry as dust after you've tasted the reality."

A wave of heat moved through her that had nothing to do with the blazing logs in the hearth. She could feel her breasts swell and the muscles of her stomach clench, as memories tumbled back to her. She reached hurriedly for the first tape and threw it into the fire. The blaze flared as the plastic entered the flames.

"You'd better throw them all into the fire at one time." Sabin grimaced. "That plastic burning is going to smell terrible."

"I know. I burned the originals, remember?" She threw the five remaining tapes into the fire and stood looking down at them. "Thank you, Sabin."

"You persist in thinking I'm being generous," he said roughly. "I wanted those damn tapes destroyed as much as you did. I hate the thought of Ben behind the camera taking those pictures. It used to eat into me like acid."

"Then why did you look at them?" she asked haltingly, her gaze on the fire.

"You," he said simply. "It was the only way I could have you."

He stood two feet away from her, but she felt as if he were touching her, stroking her as he had that night. She felt a tingling between her thighs, in her palms, even in the arches of her feet.

"I used to fantasize how you'd feel around me," he said thickly. "How you'd move, the sounds you'd make. How you'd smile at me."

She turned abruptly away from the fire. "I think it's definitely time we went in to dinner." She started across the room toward the door, her gaze deliberately avoiding the leather chaise lounge as she passed it. "I'm hungry."

"So am I."

Sabin's soft words rang clear in the room behind her. She tried to ignore the double entendre as she opened the door, but she found her hand was trembling on the knob.

Though she had heard no sound, Sabin was suddenly beside her at the door. "There's no use trying to run away from it," he said quietly. "Lord knows, I've tried since the first moment I saw you at the premiere. What's between us won't go away, and it won't let us go." He bowed mockingly as he gestured for her to precede him. "Time may well lessen it and familiarity dull it, but we don't know that yet, do we?"

Pain seared through her at the cynicism in his

tone. She knew he had no faith in lasting relationships. Why did his words hurt her?

An answer leapt to her mind with stunning swiftness, the same thought that had occurred to her once before. Again she instantly rejected it before it could become more than a fleeting impression. No, she *wouldn't* believe anything so outlandish and dangerous.

She didn't answer his question as she passed through the doorway leaving both the burning tapes and the disturbing memories behind her.

Sabin may have permitted the memories to be laid to rest, but he had no intention of allowing her to lessen the sexual awareness crackling between them. Although the conversation was desultory and casual during dinner and coffee afterward, Sabin's demeanor was not. He was charged with the same raw sensual intensity she had first noticed in the courtroom and that first night at Kandrahan. Now, as then, she found herself drawn mothlike toward its burning glow.

But she mustn't be drawn to him, she thought desperately. Everything that was sensible and practical in her character shouted at the folly of becoming involved with Sabin Wyatt.

But wasn't she already involved? He had dominated her thoughts as well as her life for the past three weeks. How was she to cast him out now?

"Stop frowning," Sabin said roughly as he set his coffee cup down in the saucer with a clatter. "I'm not going to hurt you."

She looked at him, startled. He had been talking

about his friend Alex Ben Raschid, and these words had come out of nowhere.

He pushed back his chair and stood up. "Come for a walk in the garden."

"I'm tired. I think I'll—"

He wasn't listening. He was already at the French doors leading to the garden. "Come on, I've had enough of this waltzing."

She slowly rose to her feet, her heart pounding hard, erratically. "I can't imagine you waltzing. It wouldn't suit you at all," she said with an effort at lightness. "Perhaps a vigorous polka like the one in *The King and I* but not—" She broke off as she remembered the underlying sensuality in that dance between the King of Siam and his Anna, but it was too late. She could see by the arrested expression on Sabin's face that he too recognized the similarity.

"Oh, yes." He held out his hand. "We both know what's been going on tonight. I'm not good at hiding my feelings, and you've been getting more nervous by the minute. Let's clear that up right now."

She moved slowly toward him. "I'm not nervous." Breathless, excited, afraid . . . but not nervous. His hand reached out and grasped her own, and she felt a charge of feeling electrify her.

He felt her stiffen and nodded. "Wrong word," he said thickly. He pulled her out into the garden, lacing their fingers together as they walked down the path. "Is it too cool for you?"

"No." She was burning. Sabin's fingers laced through hers felt outrageously intimate, as if he'd made her part of his own body as he had when he had thrust his—"It's odd how cool it gets at night in the desert, but tonight it's warm. I remember—"

"I won't hurt you," he interrupted, not looking at

her. "I . . . care about you. Even if I make love to you, I won't turn into the Marquis de Sade."

"I don't want to talk about this."

"We've got to talk about it. I'll treat you very well. I'll take care of you. I'll give you anything you want."

She stiffened. "I don't want anything from you."

"Lord, I know that. I'm saying all the wrong things." He looked down at their joined hands. "Can't you feel it? This is *right*."

She did feel it, and it frightened her. She felt as if she were being swept away from all order and safety. "For me to become your mistress? Being a courtesan isn't one of my ambitions."

"For you to belong to me." He stopped on the path, his bold features harsh, strained in the moonlight. "Lord, Mallory, stop fighting it." He framed her face in his hands and looked down at her. "I'll be so good to you. I'll take such good care of you. Give me a chance. Don't go away from me."

Tenderness rose in her, sunlight warm, achingly sweet. All through his childhood people had left Sabin, passing in and out of his life, leaving him guarded. His fingers were moving over her face, caressing her throat, and the tenderness merged with desire. She instinctively threw back her throat to invite more of his touch.

He went still. "Mallory?" His hands closed gently around her throat, manacling her as he had that first night. "Yes?"

Dear heavens, what was she thinking about? She had been swept into one disastrous marriage by emotion, and she was allowing herself to be caught up again. She wasn't tough enough to take on Sabin Wyatt. He would destroy her, turn her inside out, make her—

His mouth was covering her own, coaxing her lips apart for his tongue. "Say yes," he muttered. "Say yes, Mallory."

His big body was trembling against her, and it was that sign of vulnerability more than the lust searing through her at his touch that brought surrender.

Her arms slid around his shoulders. "Yes," she whispered.

"Lord." The word was a groan, deep in his throat. His arms crushed her to him, his mouth hot, working as he pressed kisses on her face and throat. "You won't regret . . . I need you so." He lifted his head. "Now." He was pulling her down the path away from the palace.

"Sabin, where—"

"Here." He stopped at the bench in the enclosed, filigreed arbor. "No one can see us here." His hands were shaking as he began to unfasten her gown. "Though I don't know if I'd care if they could." He pushed the bodice of the gown down and gazed at her naked breasts, dappled with the moonlight drifting through the lacy filigreed panels of the enclosure. "Yes, I would."

His big hands cupped her breasts weighing them gently as his thumbs caressed the taut nipples. "Only for me." His gaze lifted to her face. "For heaven's sake, don't tell me you want to go back to the house."

"No." She swallowed to ease the tightness of her throat. Her breasts felt ripe and heavy in his palms, and fire was exploding through her bloodstream with her every breath. "Though we might as well go back unless you *hurry*."

He looked down at her in surprise and then laughed with boyish exuberance. "I'll hurry." His hands pushed down her gown, letting it fall to the ground. He began to unclothe her as quickly as possible. "If I can keep my hands from shaking."

Her hands were shaking too as she pushed the coat from his shoulders. "Let me help."

"We'd only get in each other's way." His voice was hoarse as he pulled off the last of her undergarments and tossed them aside. He took a step back and stood there looking at her. "Dear heaven, you're beautiful." He lifted her so that she was standing on the bench. "Stay there and let me look at you while I get rid of these clothes."

"I feel . . . awkward." The bench was cold beneath her bare feet, but that was the only part of her that was chilled. She could feel Sabin's gaze on her breasts, on the curls that encircled her womanhood as if they were a burning touch.

"You don't look awkward." Sabin's beautiful, rich voice came out of the darkness across the path. "You look like an exquisite statue that I've commissioned for my garden. But moonlight is too cold for you. We'll come here tomorrow and see how you look in the sun." He stepped forward from the shadows, and a ray of moonlight revealed the powerful muscularity of his nudity. There was nothing statuelike about Sabin, she thought. His masculinity was as earthy as his excitement and lust were palpable. His arms slid around her, and he buried his face in her abdomen, his warm tongue touching, tasting her flesh. "I'm hurting." He whispered. "Help me, Mallory."

Her awkwardness and shyness melted away as tenderness spread through every atom of her being. "We'll help each other." She smiled lovingly as her arms went around his brawny shoulders.

He lifted her and sat down on the bench, setting

her astride his lap. "Yes." He kissed her deeply as he slid her slowly onto his manhood, stretching, filling her. He groaned, his chest rising and falling with every breath. "We'll . . . help . . . each—" He broke off as he began moving her, plunging upward in a fever of need.

Madness, fullness, satiety, hunger.

Sabin was the same, yet totally different. Or was it she who was different? No drugs dulled the pleasure he brought her with each movement, no reluctance marred her surrender.

She found herself moaning, whimpering as the tension mounted to unbearable heights.

"More." Sabin muttered into her ear. "Talk to me. You like this?"

"Yes." Her nails dug into his shoulders. "But I can't—" She gasped as he rotated his hips while holding her deeply captive. "Sabin!"

"Never mind. I like to hear those little sounds better than words anyway."

He heard many of those cries in the next few minutes, and when the climax of feeling came she had to bite her lips to keep from screaming with pleasure.

She collapsed against him, without breath, gasping, trembling.

His hands caressed her bare back, soothing, petting her as he did when he held her in his arms during those long afternoon naps. However, there was nothing companionable or sexless in his stroking now. Blatant possession and sensuality imbued every touch. "Are you all right?" he asked in a low voice as soon as he could get his breath.

She nodded jerkily, not lifting her head from his shoulder.

He loosened her hair from its chignon, letting it flow down her back, his fingers tangled in the thick tresses.

"Shouldn't . . . I get off you?"

"No." He lifted her head and kissed her lingeringly. "We may spend every evening like this."

She shook her head.

"You don't like the idea." He took two silky tresses and pulled them forward to wrap them around her nipples. "Isn't that pretty?" He lowered his head, and his teeth gently tugged at one nipple.

She felt a tingle of heat move through her. Dear heaven, she was beginning to want him again. "I need to talk to you."

"Go ahead." He sucked delicately. "I'm listening."

"I can't think when . . ." She pushed him away and stood up. She immediately felt vulnerable and alone, but that was better than the helpless desire he seemed capable of stirring in her. She picked up his tuxedo jacket from the bench across the path and slipped it on.

"Now that you've removed temptation from my path, will you come back and let me hold you?"

"Not right now." She sat down on the bench across the path. "We have to understand each other. I didn't say I'd become your mistress, Sabin."

He stiffened. "You said yes."

"I said yes to this." Her gesture included both themselves and their situation. "I'm not about to become something I'm not, just because I find you sexually compatible."

"Compatible?" He laughed mirthlessly. "That's a lukewarm word for what we share. Come back and let me demonstrate just how compatible we can be."

She clutched the jacket more tightly around her.

"Very well, it was more than compatible, but I won't let it change my life. I've had it with emotional roller coaster rides."

"You think you're just going to walk away from me?"

"No." She moistened her lips with her tongue. "Not yet."

"When?"

"Three months, if you're agreeable to my terms." She tried to keep her voice steady as she continued, "I think that's fair since Carey says that's the length of your usual affairs. The film company should be through here in Sedikhan by that time."

"You still intend to make the film?"

"Of course, I'll leave tomorrow for Marasef. I'll be busy working, but we should have some time together if you'd like to come to Marasef occasionally."

She heard him mutter a curse under his breath. "I'm not accustomed to sharing, Mallory."

"Take it or leave it."

He was silent. "I have no intention of leaving you or letting you leave me," he said softly. "So, you damn well know I'm going to accept your proposition."

She had hoped, but she hadn't known. She desperately wanted something to remember when Sabin left her, even if it was only a few precious months. When he did leave her, she must have something to hold on to through the darkness to follow. Her work, her independence, her pride would remain intact if only he didn't guess the truth she had discovered a moment before when he had taken her in his arms. "I hoped you'd agree, it was the wisest way to handle—"

"I gave up wisdom along with that two hundred thousand dollars I paid for those tapes," he interrupted harshly. "I don't give a damn what's sensible at the moment. Go to Marasef if you have to, but you can bet your life I'll be there." He stood up and crossed the path in two long steps. "But you're not in Marasef tonight, and I intend to make the most of your undivided attention." He slipped his coat from her shoulders and pulled her into his arms. "I trust you agree?"

"I agree." She closed her eyes as Sabin's head lowered toward her. Perhaps it wasn't the real thing, she thought desperately. Perhaps this wasn't the same feeling her parents had for each other. Perhaps, like her affection for Ben, it would fade for her in three months time as it would for Sabin. She would be able to do this, she could strike a balance, Mallory told herself.

And, since she was a good actress, if she was very careful, Sabin would never know she loved him.

Six

The dew on the petals of the spray of gardenias shimmered in the sunlight.

Mallory raised herself on one elbow and reached out to gently touch the flower on the pillow next to her.

"I know a red rose is traditional, but I've always thought roses were commonplace." Sabin sat down on the bed beside her. He was already dressed in jeans and a loose white shirt, his brown hair water-darkened to a shade near black. "And you're definitely not commonplace."

"I do like roses," she said drowsily as she picked up the gardenias. "But these are exquisite."

"And so are you." He lowered his head to brush her bare shoulder with his lips.

She was surprised at the ripple of heated response his touch ignited in her. They had come together innumerable times during the night. Their lovemaking had been frantic, feverish, insatiable . . . leaving them exhausted and replete. Yet now as she looked at him, she felt the familiar quickening of her body.

He lifted his head to look at her, a faint flush mantled his cheeks, his light eyes luminous. "The garden's beautiful this morning. Why don't we go and see how you look in the sunlight?"

The color flew to her cheeks as she remembered how he had posed her on the bench last night. "It's broad daylight, and someone might come."

"I could send them all away from the palace for the day." He slowly pulled the sheet down to bare her to the waist, his gaze on her breasts. "Never mind, I'd never make it to the garden. We'll go there later."

Mallory felt her nipples hardening beneath his stare and a hot tingling starting between her thighs. She drew a shaky breath and pulled the sheet back up to her chin. "We don't have time. I have to leave. Marasef . . ."

He became still. "You can go to Marasef tomorrow."

She slowly shook her head.

His lips twisted. "You're a hard lady."

"If I stay today, I'd only have to face leaving again tomorrow."

"You don't have to leave at all." He said with scarcely contained violence. "Dammit, this role isn't going to make or break your career. *Stay* with me."

The temptation was nearly irresistible. She could stay here, and Sabin would give her protection and passion. The nights and days of lovemaking would surely bring them closer in mind as well as body. Perhaps she would be able to make Sabin love her as she did him. She opened her lips to tell him she would stay and then hesitated. But what if those days with her brought him only boredom, while she became even more hopelessly in love with him? She closed her mouth and again shook her head. "I can't."

"Why the hell not?"

"I told you the reasons last night. Let's not argue, Sabin."

"Why should we argue?" He stood up, his movements jerky and impatient. "After all, I'm getting what I want; three months in bed with Mallory Thane. Providing you can fit me into your schedule." He strode toward the door. "Get dressed. I'll arrange to have a car drive you to Maraset."

Mallory flinched as the door slammed behind him.

Her emotions felt as raw and bleeding as if they had been put through a shredding machine. She had made the right decision, she told herself. The only way she was going to survive those three months was if she kept Sabin only on the periphery of her life. The sexual chemistry between them was too strong. Last night had proved to her that he could dominate her effortlessly in bed, and, if she remained at Kandrahan, they would probably spend a good portion of the next three months making love.

No, it was only sensible for her to go back to the world that would still have a place for her when her relationship with Sabin was over.

She threw back the sheet, jumped out of bed, and started toward the bathroom. The room was blurring before her eyes.

What a pity that all the good sense in the world couldn't keep the tears from stinging her eyes.

"Hello, Omar." Mallory smiled at the big man holding the car door as she settled herself on the backseat of the limousine beside Carey.

"Kandrahan," he pronounced with a sunny smile as he slammed the car door shut and started around the back of the car toward the driver's seat.

"No, Marasef." Mallory turned to Carey. "Oh, dear, that language barrier again. We're not going to be driving in circles and come back here are we?"

Carey shook his head. "Sabin gave him his orders this morning. You'll end up at the right place." He paused. "If you're sure Marasef is the right place for you. Sabin wasn't overly pleased."

"I have my own life to live." She looked straight ahead. "I won't become some kind of harem girl for Sabin's amusement. It's going to be difficult enough starting my life over."

"Some women would say life with Sabin would be easier than starting off on your own again."

"Some people aren't me," Mallory said crisply. She changed the subject. "Where's the location in Marasef?"

"It's at an old abandoned airport on the city's outskirts. It was used by the allies in World War II. They've even managed to unearth some old bombers from the aviation scrap yards that are still flyable. Several buildings can be converted to sets, and there's an officers' club that they're planning on using as the café. Some of the exterior shots will have to be done in the city but the rest—"

"You didn't say good-bye."

Sabin swung open the door of the car and looked inside at her. His gray-blue eyes were as steely as his tone. "Or perhaps you didn't think I deserved that courtesy."

Mallory tensed and then forced her muscles to relax. "I thought we'd said our good-byes." She smiled with an effort. "Besides, I'll be seeing you in Marasef in a few days, won't I?"

"You're damn right you will." He stood looking at her for a moment. "Take care of her, Carey. Be sure the Global people know they'll answer to me if they give her any trouble."

"No!" Mallory said sharply. "No more favors. From now on I'm on my own."

Sabin scowled and repeated, "Take care of her, Carey." He slammed the door and motioned for Omar to start the engine before striding back into the palace.

"In the middle again." Carey grimaced. "I should be getting accustomed to the balancing act by now."

"No more favors." Mallory enunciated each word as Omar drove out of the courtyard. "There's going to be enough resentment leveled at me on the set. Favoritism by the owner of the company is hard to swallow by professionals who have worked their buns off to get their own roles."

"You've worked hard yourself."

"No favors."

"Okay," Carey said reluctantly. "But when Sabin shows up on the set, you won't get the same cooperation. He doesn't believe in sitting back and letting someone else run the show when things aren't going well."

Four hours later Mallory had to admit things definitely weren't going well.

"You can't stay here," Carey said positively as his gaze went over the interior of the tiny mobile home. Stained and chipped linoleum covered the floor, the furniture consisted of one dilapidated easy chair and a lumpy-looking couch that obviously did double duty as a bed. No kitchen, not even a hot plate, and the only lighting appeared to be provided by a bare bulb hanging from the ceiling. "For Lord's sake, it doesn't even have air-conditioning. You'll fry in this climate."

"These are the quarters I've been given. This is where I stay. It will be cooler in the evening." Mallory wiped the perspiration from her nape with her handkerchief as she glanced at the stained walls of the shower in the tiny bathroom. "I hope."

"I'll speak to the director. All the other mobile homes we saw on the grounds had air-conditioning units. There must be some mistake."

"No mistake." Mallory smiled grimly. "They have to accept me, but they don't have to make me comfortable. They're probably hoping I'll give up and go back to New York. Well, I'll be damned if I'll do it. Tell Omar to bring in my suitcases."

"Mallory, Sabin's not—"

"I can't worry about what Sabin will like. Right now, my first priority is Peter Handel, the director."

"He's responsible for this?"

"Probably. The director's responsible for everything once the cameras start rolling. He evidently doesn't like the idea of having me pushed down his throat."

Carey gave a low whistle. "Then we may have a new director when Sabin arrives on the scene."

"Why? Handel is brilliant and can make the picture something pretty special. I'm going to like working with him."

"If he doesn't eat you for breakfast."

"I'm going to see that he doesn't." She turned and ran down the three steps. "Stay here. I think I'll have my first confrontation with him and get it over with."

"I'll go with you."

She shook her head. "They know you're Sabin's assistant, and it will make it worse for them to see you hovering over me." She turned and smiled at him. "If you want to help, be here when I get back. I may need to see a friendly face. It looks like it's going to be pretty chilly around here for the next few days."

"Not in this trailer," Carey said dryly.

"True." Mallory waved and set off across the airfield toward the location where she had spotted Peter Handel lining up shots for his storyboard when she and Carey had gone to see the location manager about her quarters. One could hardly miss the blaze of the director's wild red-gold hair as he lounged high above the ground on the seat of a tall crane. She had never met Peter Handel, but she recognized the small, plump man from his pictures in the tabloids. He was only twenty-six, one of Hollywood's wunderkinds, and looked like a curly-haired cherub in tennis shoes with his plump cheeks and round blue eyes. But the words coming through the megaphone, as he was swung back and forth across the sky, were far from angelic. Handel was obviously not in good temper.

Mallory waited patiently until the crane descended and then walked quickly across the tarmac toward him. "Mr. Handel, I wonder if I could have a word with you."

Handel turned to gaze at her and then smiled wolfishly. "Well, if it isn't the beauteous Mallory Thane. We've been waiting a week for you." His smile widened. "I don't like to wait."

"I was ill." She met his gaze directly. "I'm very sorry. I am prepared. I've been rehearsing for the past three weeks."

"Not under my direction," he said softly. "I like four weeks of rehearsal before the cameras roll, and I'm not going to have it. This role's damn important to the picture, and I won't have it ruined by a play-girl who'd rather sleep with her boss than show up on the set."

The color flooded Mallory's cheeks. "I was ill," she repeated. "You'll find I'm very reliable and know my job."

"We'll see." He turned toward the camera on the crane. "Your first scene is tomorrow morning. Report to makeup at five A.M. Go see Josh Abrams about your quarters."

"I already did. I'm settled in."

He turned back, his angelic face wreathed in malice. "I do hope you'll be comfortable. Naturally, we would have given you something a little more palatial if we'd known when you'd deign to show up."

"I'm every bit as comfortable as you wanted me to be." She grimaced ruefully. "I've had worse."

He looked disappointed. "You may change your mind by the end of the day. It gets hot as blazes about four."

"I won't be in the trailer enough for it to matter. When I'm not needed on the set, I intend to watch you work."

"Me?"

"You're brilliant," she said simply. "I think the work you did in *Blackout* was fantastic."

His gaze narrowed on her face. "Why should an actress be interested in a director's work?"

"Because I love movie-making. I think it's the premiere art form of our century." She shrugged. "Even if the public gradually learns to accept me again, the good roles for actresses are few and far between. If I can't work in front of the camera, I'll try to work behind it."

His face was impassive. "It won't work."

"What?"

"You're trying to soften me up, but I've been conned by experts, hot stuff."

"I'm telling you the truth," she said. "But I know I can't convince you with words."

"That's perceptive," he drawled. "You can't convince me at all, Miss Thane. I know you're billed as a vamp, but I'm not susceptible. Go back to Wyatt where your talents are appreciated."

"They'll be appreciated here. It will just take hard work and time."

He smiled his evil, cherubic smile. "Honey, you don't know what hard work is." He motioned to the crane operator. "But it will be my honor and privilege to show you." Before she could reply, the crane lifted him soaring into the sky.

Mallory sighed as she watched Handel resume lining up the shots from his storyboard.

"Do any good?"

She turned to see Carey standing beside her. "Not much. It's going to be a tough fight."

"How about dinner? You're obviously going to need your strength, and I know the best restaurants in Marasef."

"Sounds wonderful." She deliberately turned away from the crane bearing Handel and tried to dismiss him from her thoughts. "Give me a half hour to shower and change." She thought of something. "Will you place a call for me to James in New York while I'm in the shower? I don't want him to read me the riot act for not calling again."

"My pleasure." Carey took her elbow. "It's my job

to smooth your path, and you're certainly not letting me do it in any other way."

"You're exhausted." Carey's worried gaze searched Mallory's face. "You've been working on this damn scene for ten hours."

"Handel is a perfectionist."

"So I've noticed, but he's not this hard on the other actors." Carey said grimly. "For the past four days he's run you ragged. You look worse now than when you first came to Kandrahan."

"I'm fine." She leaned back against the wall of the café and closed her eyes. Lord, her feet hurt in these four-inch heels. She wished she could sit down, but she didn't want to chance mussing the gown and giving Handel another excuse to rake her with his forked tongue. "Just a little tired."

"You're losing weight again. I heard the wardrobe mistress grumbling about having to alter your gown." His gaze went over Mallory's slender figure in the black gown. Her bare arms and shoulders gleamed pale and fragile, though the transparent black nylon and the exquisite gold-beaded flowers half-veiling each breast gave her a graceful, exotic allure. "Sabin's going to raise hell."

"Sabin's not here." Mallory opened her eyes and straightened away from the wall as she heard Peter Handel impatiently shouting her name. "They're ready for me again."

"Mallory, let me talk to that little bastard."

"Not on your life." Mallory pushed back her hair with a shaky hand. "He won't keep on with this when he sees I'm not going to break. He's too professional to waste production money."

She ignored Carey's muttered curses as she wound her way around the tables in the café to the bandstand. She could have uttered a few curses herself, she thought grimly. Handel might be brilliant but he was positively diabolic when it came to devising ways to annoy and exhaust her. Dear heavens, she was tired. She was still having trouble sleeping at night without those blasted pills, and she no longer had the solace of those afternoon naps in Sabin's arms.

A jab of pain shot through her, and she quickly blocked the thought of those weeks at Kandrahan. She was having enough trouble coping with the problems here without looking wistfully over her shoulder.

"Ah, Miss Thane." Handel's eyes widened with pretended surprise as they scanned her face. "You look a trifle wilted. Have we been working you too hard?"

"No." Mallory kept her voice steady.

"Then are we ready to begin again?"

"Yes."

"Good." Handel smiled nastily. "Do see if you can keep from sounding like a breathy Marilyn Monroe while you're singing the song, won't you? In the forties singers relied on voice and melody."

"I'm sorry. I'll try to do better."

For an instant Handel looked disconcerted before he turned away with a shrug. "I'm sure we'll all appreciate it. This scene has been a headache from the first take."

He stopped her three times during the song "I'll Be Seeing You" with scathing criticisms and twice during the dialogue afterward with Brett O'Neal, the male lead, who played a pilot with whom the singer was having an affair.

"No fire," Handel said bluntly. "Nothing, Miss Thane. The man has to have some reason to forget his sweetheart back home and have an affair with you. The way you're playing her, Renee might just as well be a blank sheet of paper."

"I'll do it over," Mallory said.

"The hell you will," Sabin said from the corner of the room.

Mallory's eyes closed for an instant. Not now. Sabin couldn't have shown up at a worse possible moment. Her lids flicked open, and she ignored both Sabin's words and the man himself. Her gaze never left Handel's face. "I'm sorry, I'll do it again. I'll try to do it right this time."

"No." Sabin was striding across the set toward them. Dressed in a white tropical Giorgio Armani suit, he looked both formidable and blatantly out of place on the set. "Call it a day, Handel."

"And just who are—" Handel broke off as he gazed at Mallory's face. "Ah, Global's new owner? You'll find my contract gives me protection from interference from executives, Wyatt."

"Go away, Sabin," Mallory said between her teeth.

"And let you collapse?" Sabin asked. "Carey should have called me when he saw this—"

"Carey had no business telling you of my problems." She whirled to face him. "Get the hell off the set. I'll do this scene until the director says it's right. That's my job." Her eyes blazed at him. "And by heaven, I'll do it."

Sabin gazed at her a moment, a montage of expressions flickering over his face. He whirled on his heel and stalked off the set toward the corner where Carey waited.

Mallory turned back to face Handel. "Where do you want me to start?"

A thoughtful frown furrowed Handel's round face. "What?"

"Do I start with the song again?"

His arrested expression vanished, and Handel shook his head. "No." He turned away. "We'll call it a wrap."

"No, I want to finish. These shots are costing Global money."

The faintest smile curved Handel's lips as he looked back at her. "Why be such a perfectionist, Miss Thane? I've decided the third take of the day was quite adequate." He waved his hand at the crew. "Wrap."

The third take had been done at eleven this morning. It was now almost eight in the evening.

Mallory watched in astonishment as Handel strolled away with matchless aplomb. If she hadn't been so exhausted she would have been furious.

No, she was too relieved and grateful to be angry. She was still on trial with the director, but she had an idea the biggest battle had just been fought and won.

"May I speak now?"

Mallory turned to see Sabin standing a few feet away.

"Not if you're going to yell at me. I've had my fill of coping with temperament today."

"So Carey's been telling me." Sabin's expression was inscrutable as he stared at her. "I have no intention of yelling at you."

She gazed at him warily. "Or lecturing me?"

"It's useless. You'd only ignore me." He took her

elbow. "I'll feed you instead. Come on, let's go to your trailer and—"

"I have to shower and change," she said quickly. "Why don't you go over to the commissary tent with Carey, and I'll meet you there in an hour?"

He stiffened. "You're trying to get rid of me."

Hurt threaded the words, and Mallory felt a pang of remorse. "No, I just wanted to avoid . . ." She sighed resignedly. "Oh, what the devil, let's go." She turned and moved across the café set toward the door.

Sabin's face was expressionless as he gazed around the tiny trailer. "I've seen elevators larger than this."

"You're exaggerating."

"No air-conditioning."

"Now, that's not an exaggeration." Mallory could feel the perspiration already beading her throat though they had just entered the mobile home. "It's hotter in here than it is outside. Why don't you wait out there while I—"

"I'll stay here." He spun her around and began to unfasten the black gown. "Get in the shower. I'll make reservations at a restaurant on the bay where the food is good and the air-conditioning is ice-cold."

"It sounds like heaven."

"Just civilization." His lips tightened. "Something you've clearly been doing without for the last few days. I suppose you won't let me take you to a hotel for the night?"

She shook her head as she moved toward the bathroom. "No favors."

"I didn't think so. Why are you limping?"

She lifted the hem of the gown to reveal the four-inch platform heels.

"Christ, come here." He didn't wait for her to obey him but took two steps, picked her up in his arms, and plopped her down on the couch. "Were these hooker's shoes Handel's idea too?" He unfastened the ankle straps of the shoes, slipped them off her feet, and began to massage the toes and instep of her left foot.

"No, wardrobe's." She closed her eyes and sighed blissfully. Even through the stocking his warm, strong fingers felt wonderfully soothing. "And they're not hooker's shoes. Women wore these platform sandals frequently in the forties, and all the clothes have to be authentic. The shoes are okay as long as I don't wear them for long periods."

"Like twelve hours in a row."

"Carey has a very big mouth."

"Don't go to sleep. You have to eat first."

"I'm not asleep. I'm just about to purr. Do you know that some people believe you can cure any pain in your body by manipulating certain muscles in your feet?"

"No." He started massaging her right foot. "And I don't believe I'm in danger of becoming a disciple."

"I am."

"Then it's time I stopped and shoved you into a cold shower."

"What a terrible thought." She languidly opened her eyes to see him gazing down at her, his face only a short distance away from her own. For an instant she thought she saw something wistful, almost vulnerable, in his face before it became inscrutable again.

He abruptly stood up and set her carefully on her

feet. "Start with a warm shower to loosen up your muscles and then finish with a cold spray." He turned and picked up the receiver of the phone on the table. "Don't come out for fifteen minutes."

She didn't tell him the hot water heater didn't work.

"What do you want to wear?"

"I don't know. I'll decide later."

He looked over his shoulder, his glance raking her shadowed eyes and luminous pallor. "I'll choose." He smiled crookedly. "It shouldn't be hard to find your closet in this hot box."

She hesitated. "You're being very kind. I thought you'd be angry with me."

"Why? You were right. I'd have been mad as hell if you'd strolled into a board meeting and told me I was too tired to function and had to come home."

"Even if you were?"

" 'It's my job.' " He quoted her words. "You don't quit until the work is done."

"Right."

"So I'll just have to make sure the 'work' runs smoothly so that we don't have another confrontation that causes you to verbally pin my ears back."

"It will go better on the set from now on."

"I think you're right. Handel respects you now." His lips curved in a slow, warm smile. "And so do I."

Her heart leapt, and joy swept through her, miraculously banishing the weariness. A brilliant smile lit her face as she hurried toward the bathroom. "I'll be out in a minute."

"Don't hurry." He paused. "You did, you know."

She looked back at him inquiringly.

"Pinned my ears back." He smiled faintly. "You

blazed up and let me have it with both barrels. Not a calm, pacifying thought to be seen on the horizon."

"You seem very pleased about it."

"Oh, I am. It's not all I could hope for, but I think it bodes well for the future." He began to dial the number on the phone. "A full fifteen minutes in that shower. You need the extra time to get the kinks out of all those muscles."

Seven

Dinner proved to be a wonderfully relaxing affair. The lobster was delicious, the air-conditioning all that Sabin had claimed, and Sabin, himself, completely companionable and undemanding.

When they arrived back at the trailer, he unlocked the door and handed her the key. "I'd offer to share that bed of nails, but I doubt if either one of us would sleep. We'd be on top of each other, and you can be sure more than the springs would be poking at you."

She found herself giggling like a teenager. "I think you're just too fond of your air-conditioned hotel room to give it up for my humble abode."

His smile faded. "After five days away from you? Not likely. I'm so hot I wouldn't even notice the temperature."

She inhaled sharply as she met his gaze. She had a sudden vision of herself astride Sabin, her knees on the garden bench, his hands on her hips sealing her to him as he plunged wildly upward. "I've . . .

gotten used to the springs poking me. I'm very adaptable."

He took an impulsive step forward and then stopped. "No, I don't want you adaptable." His index finger touched her left cheek. "I want you horny as hell." His finger moved down to test the rapid pounding of the pulse in the hollow of her throat. "And you're too involved in this struggle with Handel to give me the response I want right now. Work out your problems." He kissed her lightly on the nose. "I'll be around."

With a puzzled frown, she watched him walk away. His entire attitude since she had turned on him in the café bewildered her. She knew he could be kind, but as patience was not his forte, she had expected him to accept her invitation.

She made a face as she opened the door of the trailer. Carey had said she looked tired, and Handel had used the word wilted. Not descriptions to inspire passion in any man. Maybe Sabin hadn't desired her as much as he had said and wanted an excuse not to spend the night with her.

She just hoped Sabin would keep his word and be around when she was in better shape. Dedication to one's work was all very well, but she felt very much alone as she climbed the steps and shut the door of the trailer.

The next day on the set revealed that the worst was indeed over. Handel worked Mallory hard, and his manner was not warm, but she saw only fleeting glimpses of the biting sarcasm that had previously characterized his attitude.

Two days later, a hot plate appeared mysteriously in the trailer.

The next day when she returned from the set, a window unit air-conditioner had been installed.

At the end of the week the dilapidated couch had been replaced by a new one that opened into a comfortable bed.

Handel gave no indication he was responsible for any of the changes, and Mallory discreetly made no mention of their miraculous appearance in her small domain.

"The lap of luxury," Carey said. He sighed as he stretched his legs out before him and leaned his head on the cushioned back of the couch. "Though I believe I was getting used to those broken springs."

"I wasn't." Mallory came out of the tiny bathroom after dressing for dinner. "You didn't have to sleep on them."

"That's true." He met her gaze. "Neither did you. You know Sabin would have—"

"I haven't seen Sabin lately." She tried to keep her tone casual. "Has he left Sedikhan?"

Carey shook his head. "He's been having meetings with the reigning sheikh. I've seen him almost every day." He grinned. "Shall I tell him you inquired?"

"No," she said quickly. "I only wondered why . . . He said he'd be around."

His grin faded. "I told you Sabin couldn't stand around idle when things aren't going to his satisfaction. He's very protective of you, and I'd bet he knew the only way he could allow you to fight your own battles was not to be there to see them."

Happiness and relief flowed through her. "You think so?"

He nodded. "Now that you've slain your dragon, he'll be knocking on your door."

A knock sounded at the trailer door.

Carey chuckled. "Right on cue." He threw up his hands. "As God is my witness, I swear I didn't stage this."

Her heart gave a leap. Sabin?

She jumped up, crossed the room in three strides, and opened the door.

James Delage stood on the grass outside the trailer looking as cool and Brooks-Brothers-neat in the hot Mideastern sun as he had when she had last seen him in New York.

She blinked, gazing at him in disbelief. "James?"

He smiled. "The same. Don't I get a hug after traveling all this way?"

Mallory flew down the steps and into his arms. "James, what on earth are you doing here?"

He kissed her cheek, his arms holding her close. "You know Gerda and I didn't like the idea of your going to this outlandish place. We were worried about you."

"So you came halfway around the world to check up on me?"

"Are you kidding?" He shook his head ruefully. "You know I couldn't afford a trip like this if it wasn't on an expense account. Sedikhan Oil threw some business my way, and I let them pick up the tab." He kissed her lightly on the lips again. "I thought I'd kill two birds with one stone. Put Gerda's mind at rest and dip my toes into international law."

"I'm glad you did." Mallory hugged him again. "Did you bring Gerda with you?"

He shook his head. "Sedikhan Oil wouldn't shell out for my spouse."

"Really?" Carey stood in the doorway looking down at them. "We've dealt with them before and found them very generous to their employees when they bring them overseas for any length of time."

Mallory felt James stiffen against her as he looked overhead at Carey. "Who the devil are you?"

Carey looked surprised at James's belligerence. "Carey Litzke."

"Carey's connected with Global Cinema," Mallory said. "He acts as a liaison between the production company and Wyatt Enterprises. This is James Delage, Carey."

"Hi," Carey said casually. "I understand you and Mallory are great friends."

"Yes." James didn't smile. "Very good friends."

Mallory stepped back out of James's embrace. "We were just going to dinner. Come with us?"

James's gaze was still fixed coldly on Carey. "Delighted."

"Good." Carey came down the steps and closed the door. "Wyatt Enterprises has a good deal of clout with Sedikhan Oil. Maybe I could put in a word with them and ask them to bring your wife over."

"No," James said and when Mallory looked at him in surprise, he smiled easily. "I'm only going to be here for a short time, and I don't want to make waves with a new client."

Carey shrugged. "Whatever you say."

Mallory slipped an arm through each of the men's and asked eagerly. "Tell me what's happening in New York, James. It seems as if I've been gone a decade."

"Where should I start?"

"Gerda, of course."

"She's tinted her hair red." James grimaced. "And she's wearing kelly green contact lenses. She looks like a punk rocker."

Mallory laughed.

"And she's learning to play the guitar." James added, "You should hear the racket she . . ."

James dialogue went on through the drive into Marasef, dinner, and the drive back to the location. He appeared to have completely discarded his belligerence and was being charming with Mallory and courteous to Carey.

James left Mallory at the door of the trailer with an affectionate kiss and a promise to call her in the next few days. He nodded politely to Carey and strode off toward his navy blue rental car parked a short distance away.

Carey watched him walk away with a slight frown on his face. "He's different from what I imagined from Sabin's description."

"What did you expect?"

"I'm not sure. Someone older and more . . . settled. Maybe Gregory Peck in *To Kill a Mockingbird*." He grimaced. "He didn't like me being here in your trailer."

"He and Gerda are very protective of me." Mallory unlocked the door of the trailer. "I wish she could have come with him."

"Yes, it's too bad Sedikhan Oil didn't come through for him." He brushed her forehead with his lips. "Good night, Mallory. Sleep well."

"On my new deluxe couch?" She cast him a smile over her shoulder and opened the door. "It's a sure thing."

•   •   •

Mallory was instantly aware of Sabin the moment he walked onto the set the next day. He settled himself on a chair in the corner of the room, watching the proceedings with keen interest. When she had finished her scene, she came over to his corner.

He stood up. "Are you finished for the day?"

She nodded. "We're done with the café shots unless the rushes aren't up to par. In fact, my work in the picture should be finished in the next few days."

His gaze searched her face. "Are you all right? Carey says Handel's been treating you pretty well."

"Working with Handel could never be a tranquil experience, but it hasn't been hellish either." She paused, her gaze on his face. She couldn't seem to look away from him. "How have you been?"

A rare smile broke the impassiveness of his face. "Impatient." His gaze traveled slowly over her. "Did I ever tell you how much I like that gown? Sexy but romantic. Like you."

"Not Pollyanna?"

"Not tonight." He glanced around the rapidly emptying room. "Stay here. I left a picnic basket in the refrigerator at the commissary tent."

"But I have to change."

He shook his head. "Not yet. Humor me. Okay?" He touched her cheek with his index finger, and she felt the familiar tingle of response. "I've been thinking about this for awhile, and I want it to be right."

She could feel the breath catch in her throat as she looked up at him. Lord, she had missed him. She hadn't realized until this moment how hollow the days had been. "Okay."

His rare smile illuminated his face. "Great. Sit down at one of the tables and rest. I'll be right back."

She gazed after him bemusedly for a moment before turning and moving back onto the set and sitting down at one of the small damask-covered tables. She mustn't feel this excited, she told herself. It would be too difficult to face being without him if she let these moments mean too much. She deliberately tried to concentrate on her surroundings, the framed pictures of World War II aviators on the walls, the ceiling fan whirring softly, the huge lights focused on the set. . . .

It was no use, she *was* excited. She could feel the blood pounding in her veins and the exhilaration soaring through her like a wild bird.

The set was completely deserted by the time Sabin walked back into the café carrying a huge picnic basket. He stopped at the door and shot the bolt before turning to face her. "Are you hungry?"

"No."

"Neither am I." He came toward her. "Suppose we save dinner for later." He set the picnic basket on the table and foraged in its interior and brought out a tape recorder. "A little music . . ." He pressed the button on the tape recorder and the triumphant music of "Shall We Dance" poured from the small machine. "Shall we dance, Mallory?"

Mallory began to laugh helplessly. "*The King and I.* I'm sorry, your majesty, I can't dance the polka in these four-inch heels."

"I know." He fast forwarded the tape. "That was just to make you laugh and relax you. This is for us." He pressed the button, and her own husky voice soared out over the set singing "I'll Be Seeing You." "I had Carey bring a tape recorder to the set the other day." He held out his hand. "Let me hold you, Mallory."

Mallory stood up and flowed into his arms, moving languidly to the music. His body was big, comforting in its strength against her. Yet there was no real comfort in this embrace. The heated response between them was too intense to ever be soothing. It had been too long since that night at Kandrahan, and she only wanted him *closer*. She cuddled nearer and felt him stiffen against her.

"Not yet," he said thickly. "I'm trying to be romantic, dammit."

She looked up at him. His face was flushed and his lips heavy with sensuality. "Why?"

"Because you deserve it. Because I want you to look at me like you did that Greek god who played opposite you in that scene."

"That was acting."

"Well, I want the real thing," he said roughly. "I want it all."

She laughed helplessly. "And you think a romantic setting will get it for you?"

He frowned. "No?"

"No." She shook her head. "For Pete's sake, Sabin, who wants Little Lord Fauntleroy when they can have the Sheikh."

"I thought most women these days preferred the polished approach." He stopped in the middle of the dance floor. "You'd rather have me the way I am? Rough edges and all?"

A faint smile touched her lips. "Rough edges can be very . . . stimulating."

He smiled down at her. "Thank the Lord." He drew her close. "Then I can tell you that hearing your voice singing that song reminds me of the first time I saw the videotapes."

Her amusement vanished as she remembered those erotic tapes. "They do?"

He nodded against her temple. "Your voice wraps around me, pulling at me." His hands slid around her, cupping her bottom in his palms as he began to dance again. "Stroking me."

A liquid tingling started between her thighs. His big hands were a heavy, sensual weight, and every step felt like an erotic caress. "Handel . . . didn't think I did the song all that well."

"Every man in the theater audience will disagree." His hands slid up her back, unfastened the catch of the gown, and began to massage her nape. "I may decide to bury the film like Howard Hughes did *The Outlaw*."

"You wouldn't do that," she whispered. Her breasts were swelling against the gown's thin material, and she could feel the nipples harden in helpless response as his hands slid around to caress her. "Would you?"

"No." He pulled the gown down, baring her shoulders. "But only because I know I couldn't get away with it. You'd tip your hat and say good-bye."

As he was going to do, she thought sadly. But not yet. Not tonight. The thought brought a frantic urgency in its wake. She stepped back and pulled the gown down to her waist and pushed it over her hips to pool on the floor, leaving her in only a garter belt, stockings, and high heels. "I'm not wearing a hat."

He went still as his gaze traveled over her bare breasts. "You're not wearing much of anything. I don't believe that was the style in the forties." He bent forward, his mouth opening to envelope one breast. "But who am I to complain?"

She cried out and arched forward as his teeth

closed on her nipple. Fire streaked through her, the muscles clenched in her stomach. "Sabin . . ."

He lifted his head to smile down at her. "Hard edges? I'll show you hard edges." He lifted her and set her on the table. "I'm nothing but rock hard and edged. I feel as if every breath is cutting into me." He took a step back and stripped off his gray coat, jacket, tie, and shirt, his gaze fastened on her. "Take off the rest, Mallory."

She gazed at him, startled.

"No cameras. No Ben. Just me. Do it for me."

She gazed at him thoughtfully, and the realization came to her that he needed this. He had told her how jealous and tormented he had been as he had watched those blasted tapes.

"For you," she said softly. She reached down and slowly unfastened the tab holding the stocking on her left thigh.

It was different.

She had been acting the temptress when she had performed on those other tapes; there was no acting now. Every muscle of her body was charged with a desire and hunger so intense, she could feel it ripple through her with every motion as she slowly peeled off the few pieces of clothing still remaining. Sabin's gaze was hard, hot, his body tense as he watched every movement. She could feel her breasts ripen, become heavier beneath his stare, and every breath was an effort as her lungs contracted. When she was done she sat there, looking at him, her cheeks flaming with color.

"Lie down." His voice was almost guttural as his hands undid his belt.

Her eyes widened. "On the table? There's no room."

He took three steps forward and with one sweeping movement dashed the vase and candle from the table to the floor. "Now there's room." He undid her chignon, and her hair flowed down her back. "Lie down, love."

His gaze held her own as he carefully lowered her backward on the small round table, arranging her hair so that it hung in a curtain over the edge of the table. The other side of the table supported only her upper thighs.

"It's too small," she whispered.

He shook his head and brought her palm to rub his chest. "It's just right. You'll see." He widened her thighs, his thumb searching, pressing.

She cried out, her back arching up from the table.

His thumb rotated slowly. She bit her lower lip to keep from screaming with pleasure.

He drew a harsh breath. "Now stay there. Don't move. I want to look at you as I finish undressing."

He moved out of her line of view, and she could hear the rasp of his belt as he drew it through the loops. Her heart began to pound harder, and her muscles tautened with unbearable tension. She was acutely conscious of the ceiling fan whirling above her, the hot camera lights staring down at her. There was something intensely erotic about lying here before Sabin, open to him, knowing he was looking at her and yet unable to see him. The heavy weight of her hair streaming down, pulled by gravity and her position, was like a manacle holding her for his pleasure . . . and her own. She began to tremble helplessly. "Sabin?"

"Soon." She heard the soft thud of a shoe dropping somewhere across the room. "Think about it." His deep, beautiful voice reverberated in the room.

"Think about how it's going to be. How I'll feel inside you. How we'll be together."

Her jaw clenched as a burning began deep inside her. She moaned deep in her throat and moved, undulated, on the table.

She heard the sharp intake of his breath. "Lord, do you know how you look? I can't—"

"Sabin!" It was an urgent cry.

"Shh, I'm here."

He was standing over her, naked. His expression intent, his deep chest lifting and falling with the harshness of his breathing. The muscles of his stomach and thighs were tight, locked with the tension of anticipation. She wanted to reach out and run her fingers over the triangle of hair thatching his chest. She just wanted to *touch* him.

He lifted her thighs and drew her to the edge of the table. "Wrap your legs around me," he murmured, his hand cupping, squeezing her. "Hot. Lord, you're on fire. Do you know how that makes me feel?"

She knew only how it made her feel. Her legs encircled him as she started to pant, her breath coming in gasps, her head thrashed back and forth on the damask cloth. "Sabin, I need you. I can't stand—"

He sank deep, hard, thick, wonderful.

She shuddered and moistened her lips with her tongue. "Yes," she whispered. "That's what I need."

He was still, looking down at her with narrowed eyes, his nostrils flaring. His palms slid around and cupped her bottom. "Hard edged?" He lifted her high and plunged deep at the same time.

She cried out, staring up at him in mindless pleasure.

He did it again, and again, and again, his hips jerking with pistonlike regularity, sending her a hot, almost brutal message of lustful pleasure. "This is *me*. Is this what you want?"

She couldn't speak, she couldn't breathe. She felt as if every inch of her flesh was burning with the waves of pleasure going through her.

"Is it?"

"Yes . . ."

He plunged wildly, his eyes above her as glazed and mindless as her own. He touched her to the quick. "Take . . ."

The tears rolled down her cheeks as she tried to take more of him.

Searing hunger.

Pleasure.

Madness.

And, at last, completion.

Mallory couldn't stop sobbing as Sabin collapsed over her. Her arms slid around him, holding him frantically as the last rapturous spasms shuddered through them both.

"I wish you'd stop crying." Sabin's voice was uneven. "I can't be sure if I've hurt you with those tears pouring down your face."

She laughed shakily. "You didn't hurt me. It was . . ." She trailed off and shook her head. "I think I went a little crazy."

He straightened, gently patting the curls surrounding her womanhood before stepping back and leaving her. "Me, too." He lifted her to a sitting position on the table and smoothed back her hair.

The caress was poignantly familiar, peculiarly his own. How many times before had Sabin reached up and gently stroked back her hair in just that way?

He cupped her cheeks in his palms and kissed her on the mouth. "It was too long a wait. We'll have to make sure that doesn't happen again."

She looked at him dazedly. "I . . . should get dressed."

He shook his head. "Why? The door's locked and no one's going to come in. I like to look at you." He stepped closer again and took her in his arms, cuddling her, cosseting her.

She liked to look at him too. She wanted to reach out and run her palm over the flat muscularity of his stomach, the brawny tree trunk thighs. "What are we going to do now?"

He reluctantly released her and stepped back. "Eat dinner?" His eyes twinkled. "It will give us a taste of what life's like in a nudist colony."

She stood up and shook her head. "I believe in a touch of mystery." She picked up her gown and slipped it over her head. "I don't want you to get tired of me too soon."

His smile vanished. "I don't think you have to worry about that." He turned away and walked over to the table where he had set the picnic basket. "And I don't want to talk about that three-month bull right now."

Neither did she, Mallory thought with a wrenching pang. Their time together would come to an end soon enough without dwelling on it. She padded across the room toward him, her bare feet cool on the tile floor. "Aren't you going to dress?"

"No." His tone was clipped. "There's no mystique about me. What you see is what you get." He opened the basket. "And believe me, you'll be getting plenty of me from now on. I'm not about to lurk in the background any longer."

"I never asked you to stay in the background."

He took out a tray of sandwiches and a bottle of wine from the basket and set them on the table. "Eat."

She stood looking at him uncertainly.

He looked up at her and a wry smile curved his lips. "It's okay. Just a few of those sharp edges showing again. I feel a little raw."

"Why?"

He shook his head as he began rummaging in the basket again. "Never mind. I'll get over it."

Get over what? she wondered. She opened her lips to pursue the question and then closed them without asking. He was with her again, and she wanted nothing to disturb the harmony of their togetherness.

She forced a smile and stepped closer to him. "Let me help. Are there any wineglasses in that basket?"

Eight

The phone shrilled in the darkness.

Mallory murmured and burrowed closer to Sabin on the sofa bed.

The phone rang again.

Drat it, she didn't want to move, she thought drowsily. Her five o'clock wake up call would come soon enough.

The phone rang again.

"I'll get it." Sabin rolled away from her, got out of bed, and turned on the light. "It's probably a wrong number anyway."

She watched him cross to the phone on the table beneath the window. Lord, he had a fantastic tush. "Then why answer it?"

"People who ring in the middle of the night are usually under the influence or have an emergency. Either way, they don't give up easily." He picked up the receiver. "Hello." He waited and then said it again. "Hello. Who is this?"

He replaced the receiver and came back to bed. "I told you it was a wrong number. They hung up."

Mallory tensed with familiar dread before she forced herself to relax. Not here. This was Marasef, not New York.

It must have been a wrong number just as Sabin had said.

Sabin flicked off the light, lay down beside Mallory, and pulled her close. He nuzzled her temple. "It seems a shame to go back to sleep when we have only a few hours until dawn."

She chuckled. "You're already half-asleep."

"Are you impugning my stamina?"

"After last night? I wouldn't dare."

He kissed her shoulder. "Then why don't we—" He broke off and shook his head. "Sorry, I didn't think. You have to work this morning and need your rest. Go back to sleep."

"If you'd rather—"

"Oh, I'd definitely 'rather'," he said dryly. "But I'm not going to do it. I've got to learn not to be such a selfish bastard. Believe me, it's not easy for me after all these years of thinking only of myself. Now hush and go back to sleep."

They lay snuggled together, warmly, beautifully content. A short time later she could tell by Sabin's even breathing that he'd drifted off to sleep again.

Not here, Mallory thought, gazing at the shadowy shape of the telephone across the room. She was safe here in Sedikhan; safe with Sabin. The person on the other end of the line had probably not hung up immediately because he had been startled that Sabin had answered in English. She would forget all about the blasted call and go back to sleep.

But it was over an hour later before she finally fell into an uneasy doze.

For the next two days, Sabin visited the set constantly. Handel was surprisingly lenient about his presence, and a few times Mallory had actually seen him stroll over to the corner where Sabin was sitting and chat for a few moments.

"Which one of you is softening?" she asked Sabin as she joined him after the second day's shoot. "I was sure Handel would have you thrown off the set."

Sabin shrugged. "Creative temperament is all very well, but all directors know it's damn difficult to earn a living directing when the cash ceases to flow into a production. Handel's not stupid enough to cut off his nose to spite his face on future projects." He stood up and took her arm. "Finished for the day?"

"Finished, period. That was my last scene in the picture."

"Good. Now can we concentrate on—"

"Mr. Wyatt?" A young gofer boy was at Sabin's elbow. "Phone call for you on line two." He handed him the phone and pulled up the aerial before turning and hurrying back toward the set.

"I'll get out of this costume and meet you back here in forty minutes," Mallory said as Sabin pushed the button for line two and spoke into the receiver.

He nodded absently as he listened to the person on the other end of the line.

Mallory turned and began to weave her way around the cameras, careful not to trip over the thick cords snaking across the floor of the hangar.

Sabin caught up with her before she reached the door. "Let's go."

She looked at him, startled. "Now? But I told you—" She broke off as she saw his face. He was pale beneath his tan, and his lips were drawn in a grim line. "What's wrong?"

"Plenty. There's no time for you to change." He grabbed her arm and strode toward the door. "That was my office. Carey's been taken to the emergency room at Sedikhan General Hospital."

"Carey?" Mallory hurried to keep pace with him. "An accident?"

Sabin nodded curtly. "He was crossing the street in front of the Wyatt office building and was run down by a car. The bastard didn't even bother to stop."

"No," Mallory whispered, her eyes wide with horror. "Is he badly hurt?"

"I don't know." Sabin flung open the door and propelled her toward the Mercedes parked next to the hangar. "He was unconscious when the ambulance took him to the hospital." He opened the car door. "We'll just have to see."

Sabin's face was shadowed with pain, Mallory noticed with a rush of sympathy. She cared for Carey, too, but Carey was Sabin's best friend, the only person he allowed close to him. "I'm sure he'll be all right," she said gently.

"Because I want him to be all right?" Sabin asked harshly. "There aren't any guarantees in this world and very few happy endings." He slammed the car door and strode around to the driver's seat.

Mallory flinched, her hands clenching into fists on her lap. There was no reason for Sabin's words to hurt her. He hadn't been talking about them. She had known all along Sabin had little faith in the longevity of any relationship. She mustn't think about anything right now but Carey's well-being and trying to comfort Sabin's pain.

When the doctor permitted them into the tiny sterile cubicle adjoining the emergency room, Carey was sitting upright on the examining table, a half-cast on his left arm and a white bandage encircling his head.

He grinned at Sabin and waved the cast at Mallory. "How do you like my turban? Do you think you can persuade Handel to cast me as a swami in his next picture?"

Mallory breathed a sigh of relief. Carey couldn't be too badly hurt if he could still joke. "I doubt it, you don't look mysterious enough. Whoever heard of a swami with freckles?"

"Are you all right?" Sabin asked jerkily.

Carey grimaced. "I could be better. My arm's broken in two places, and I'll never play the violin again."

"If you expect me to fall for that old chestnut, you've got—" Sabin broke off and asked. "How's the head?"

"They think maybe I have a mild concussion." Carey frowned. "They want to keep me here overnight. Can't you pull some strings and get me out of here?"

"No, I can't." Sabin's tone was adamant. "If they want you here, you stay."

"You'll be sorry. Your financial empire could fall apart overnight without my brilliant insight. You don't know how valuable I am to you."

"I know." Sabin's voice was gruff. "Believe me, I know."

Carey's smile faded as he met Sabin's gaze. "I'm okay, Sabin, right as rain."

"Of course, you are." Sabin looked away from him. "I knew nothing could crunch that hard head of yours. But I should dock your wages for being stupid enough to step in front of that car."

"I didn't step in front of him," Carey protested. "I didn't even see him. I swear, Sabin, I looked both ways and there was no one coming. The bastard came roaring out of nowhere. I heard a noise behind me and caught a blur of something blue. . . ." He shrugged. "Then, cuckooland."

"You can't identify the car?"

Carey shook his head. "I didn't see anything."

"Well, someone must have seen what happened," Sabin said. "I'll talk to the police and see what I can find out." He paused before adding grimly, "I'm going to nail him."

"And I'll hand you the hammer." Carey turned to Mallory. "Wanna write on my cast? It's virgin territory."

Mallory smiled. "I'll pass."

"Sure? By tomorrow you'll have to take a number. I'm planning on searching out every gorgeous nurse in the place and have them inscribe their—"

"You'll stay in bed and rest," Sabin said. "Let them come to you."

"That's a good idea." Carey thought about it and then shook his head. "Nah, too risky. They've never lined up for my favors before."

"But now you're an object of pity," Mallory reminded him. "Nothing touches a woman's heart like the sight of a few bandages."

"Really?" Carey lay back down on the emergency table. "I do believe I'm beginning to feel weaker. Yes, much weaker. You both can run along, but you'd better send in a nurse to take my vital signs on your way out. The brunette with the long eyelashes, I think."

"Do you need anything," Sabin asked. "Besides, the brunette?"

"Not if you manage to pry me out of here by tomorrow." Carey closed his eyes. "Lord, I hate hospitals."

"You'll stay as long as the Doctor says you need to."

"I knew you'd say that." Carey didn't open his eyes. "Well, I might as well take the opportunity to do some thinking."

"For instance?"

"Just thinking," he said vaguely. "Something's been bothering me. It doesn't fit . . ."

"Rest, don't think."

"See you tomorrow, Sabin."

"Tomorrow." Sabin hesitated and then turned on his heel and left the cubicle.

Mallory followed and fell into step with him as he strode down the corridor toward the nurse's station. "He seems to be doing well."

"No thanks to the scum that hit him," Sabin said. "He could have lay there in the street and bled to death or been run over by another car for all that lowlife cared."

"What do we do now?"

"I'm going to talk to the doctor and make sure they're not keeping anything from Carey." Sabin glanced down at Mallory. "And then I'm going to put you in a taxi and send you back to the location. I want to go to the police station and see if they have any more information about the car that hit him."

"I'll go with you."

"No," Sabin said. "That's not necessary. I'll see

you back at the location." He caught sight of the doctor who had shown them in to see Carey and strode quickly toward the desk.

Mallory experienced a swift jab of pain. He was closing her out. Well, why should she have expected anything else? His attitude drove home the realization that this was the real world and Sabin had never invited her to be part of it. The time he spent with her was cloaked in sensual dreams and, like a dream, would eventually fade away.

If she became his mistress, the dream would continue, and he would come to her at Kandrahan or one of his other residences around the world. They would make love, and he would leave her until the next time.

Until he decided there would be no next time.

She stood still watching him talk to the doctor, his expression intent, his gray-blue eyes narrowed with the intensity that was so much a part of him. She had seen that expression on his face countless times since she had come to Sedikhan. She had grown to know every frown, every smile, every gesture so well. What would it be like not to see Sabin ever again?

She closed her eyes tightly for an instant as the raw pain twisted inside her. Every day she spent with him he was becoming more endearingly her own. This wasn't what she felt for Ben; that had vanished almost before it began. This love was strengthening, growing until eventually it would dominate her entire world. Dear Lord, if she felt this devastated at the prospect of leaving him now, how would she be able to bear it after they had been together another two months?

Her eyes flicked open, and she drew a deep breath.

The answer was simple. She wouldn't be able to bear it. The memories wouldn't be a solace, they would be a torment. Those painful months she had known with Ben would pale in comparison.

"Ready?" Sabin was back beside her.

No, she wasn't ready. She would never be ready for what she knew now she must do. She forced a smile. "Yes, of course, I'm ready."

She let him escort her out of the hospital and put her into a taxi to take her back to the location.

Sabin didn't arrive back at her trailer until nearly eight that evening.

"Did you find out anything?" Mallory asked, her gaze searching his face.

"Too much," Sabin said wearily as he closed the door. "And not enough."

"What do you mean?"

"There were two witnesses, and neither of them could agree on the make of the car. Only that it was a dark color and small. The police are bringing them in tomorrow morning to show them pictures of different models to try and jog their memories." He paused. "But both witnesses said they believed Carey was run down deliberately. The car was parked at the curb down the street from the building and pulled away and accelerated only after Carey stepped into the street."

Mallory gazed at him in horrified bewilderment. "But who would want to hurt Carey?"

"How the hell do I know? The police lieutenant suggested it was probably someone who's trying to get to me and hasn't the nerve to attack me personally." His jaw clenched. "But I'm damn well going to find out who it was. There's no way I'm going to let anyone get away with this kind of bull."

Mallory crossed her arms over her breasts to suppress a shiver. Carey and she had both been touched by the ugliness of violence through no fault of their own. "What if they try to hurt Carey again?"

"I've told security to keep an eye on him until the police catch the nut who ran him down." Sabin met her gaze across the room. "And I've told them to put a watch over you too."

"Me?" She frowned in puzzlement. "I don't understand. It's you who should be guarded."

Sabin shook his head. "If Carey became a target because he's my friend, I don't want to risk anyone finding out I could be hurt if they attacked you."

She looked at him sadly. "And could you be hurt, Sabin?"

"What the devil do you mean? You know I—"

"Nothing," she said quickly. "I didn't mean anything." She moved toward the door of the trailer. "Let's go for a walk. I'm feeling claustrophobic in here."

"Have you eaten? Do you want to go out to dinner?"

"I had a sandwich earlier." She opened the door and stood looking out. The last glowing rays of the setting sun had painted lavender and pink shadows on the clouds on the horizon, but even as she watched, the brilliance faded into the deep purple of night. She took a deep breath of the cool evening air. "That's better. Let's walk over to the runway."

He frowned as he followed her from the trailer and closed the door. "Are you all right?"

She nodded and carefully avoided his gaze. "I'm only worried about Carey."

"But nothing else?"

"No, of course not." She threaded her fingers through his and led him away from the trailer in the direction of the tarmac a few hundred yards distant. The blue lights marched down either side of the short runway and the control tower was lit with a red warning signal, but there was no sound or sign of the activity that took place during the day. "Just walk with me. This is nice, isn't it?"

"Yes." She could feel his gaze on her in the darkness.

"I've enjoyed working on this picture." She pointed to the seven army green bombers lined up on the runway. "Just look at them. You'd never guess those planes are over forty years old. They could have landed here only an hour ago. I think I would have liked to have lived in the forties. Even though they were at war, it was a simpler life. Values were clearer then. Don't you ever want to run away from it all?"

"There's nowhere to run that you can't be found."

"That's what I mean. Back then there were . . . havens. Places and times where you could set real life aside and live for a while in blackberry winter."

He looked down at her, his face half-shadowed in the darkness. "Blackberry winter?"

"I grew up in the city, but my mother's people were farmers. I spent several summers on their farm in North Carolina when I was a child. I always remember the blackberry winters."

"What the devil is a blackberry winter?"

"In May there's usually a last cold snap before the heat of the summer comes. That's when the blackberries ripen." Her voice softened. "Dear Lord, how I loved that time."

"Better than spring?"

She nodded. "It was a time apart. The hues of the

flowers seemed more brilliant, the air was fresher, sharper, and when the early mist wreathed the fields, it was as if the earth had just been born." The wind was rising and caught a silky strand of her hair, splaying it over her cheek and mouth. She paused to pushed the strand back before she went on. "My grandfather used to say the blackberry winter was to remind us how beautiful the spring had been and how wonderful the summer to come was going to be. But I thought it was something more, a special gift that was all the more precious because it lasted such a short time and then was gone."

Sabin stopped in the middle of the runway. "I wish I could see your face."

"Why?"

"Because my instinct tells me something is damn wrong with you." His hands cupped her cheeks. "Why are you talking about havens and blackberry winters?"

"No reason." She hesitated. "I'm lying. There *is* a reason." She went into his arms and burrowed her head in his shoulder. He felt so strong and alive and *here.* "I think you need a haven, Sabin. I just hope you find it someday. I hope all your days are filled with springtime and your nights with the songs of summer."

He was silent a moment, his arms slowly tightening around her. "You're scaring the hell out of me. I don't give a damn about your havens or your seasons," he said huskily. "All I want is what we have together now." His lips covered her own with a passion that held an element of desperation.

Now. The present. No future. Just the poignant, vivid beauty of this time apart from the rest of their lives. She could feel the tears sting her eyes and was glad of the darkness as her arms slid around his neck.

"Let's go back to the trailer," he muttered between hot, hard kisses. "I want you . . ."

But only for the length of the blackberry winter.

Mallory blocked out the thought as the bittersweet pain swept through her. "Yes, let's go back now." She stepped back and turned to retrace her steps, reaching out blindly to grasp his hand. Every touch, every word, was precious now. She clung to his hand as they swiftly moved across the tarmac of the runway past the silent, ancient planes of yesterday.

Nine

A knock sounded on the door of the trailer.

Mallory tensed, her hands clenching on the pair of slacks she had been about to toss in the suitcase. Sabin?

No, it couldn't be Sabin. He had only left forty minutes before to go to the hospital to see Carey. And besides, Sabin wouldn't knock. She dropped the slacks on top of the other clothes she had hurriedly thrown in the suitcase and strode across the trailer to open the door.

James Delage grinned up at her. "How about taking pity on a stranger in a strange land and going to lunch with—" He broke off as he saw her brilliant eyes and tear-streaked cheeks. "What's wrong?"

"I'd rather not talk about it. Okay?" She smiled tremulously. "It's good to see you, James. I've been meaning to call you but—"

"Cut it out." James climbed the steps, his wide brow furrowed in a frown. "We've been friends too long for you to be polite to me. If you don't want to talk, that's fine, but no polite chitchat." His glance fell on the open suitcase on the couch. "You're going somewhere?"

She nodded. "Home. I finished up my part in the picture yesterday, and Handel told me this morning the rushes were fine." She closed the suitcase and snapped the lock. "So, it looks like I'll be seeing Gerda before you do. Do you have any messages for her?"

"You're leaving today?"

"The one o'clock flight to New York." She lifted the suitcase from the sofa and set it with the other two on the floor beside the telephone. "I just have to turn in my trailer key and then call a taxi."

"Give me the key. I'll run it over to the commissary and drop it off with someone there while you finish packing."

Mallory searched in her handbag, brought out the key, and handed it to him. "Thanks, James, I'm very grateful. Everything seems too much to cope with today."

James smiled and said lightly. "I'm just being selfish. I hate traveling alone."

She looked at him in bewilderment.

"I just dropped by to take you to lunch and say good-bye. I wound up my business with Sedikhan Oil yesterday. I was going to fly out tomorrow but now we can go together." He turned and opened the door. "We'll drop by my hotel and pick up my luggage on the way to the airport."

She frowned. "Are you sure you're not inconveniencing yourself because you think I need a shoulder to lean on? It's time you stopped playing big brother to me, James."

He glanced over his shoulder. "Don't be silly. I told

you I was just being selfish. Finish packing while I bring the car around from the parking area." He smiled. "Don't worry. You'll feel much better once you're on the plane and leaving this place behind. You don't belong here any more than I do. Once I get you back to New York, you'll see how your perspective will change. You'll stay with us for a few weeks, and Sedikhan will fade into a bad dream."

"I can't stay with you," Mallory protested. "You and Gerda don't have the room."

"We took a cottage for two months by the sea with the money from your legal fees. There's plenty of room." He made a face. "If you can stand Gerda's guitar playing."

"I can stand it." Mallory's eyes filled with tears. Leaving Sabin was proving to be agonizingly difficult, and it was good to know she wouldn't be alone in New York. "You're a very nice man, James."

"Certainly. Why else would Gerda have married me?"

He didn't wait for an answer but ran down the steps.

"You're officially sprung." Sabin propelled the wheelchair into Carey's hospital room. "I see you're already dressed. Hop out of that bed and into the chariot. That dragon at the nurse's station won't let you leave the premises under your own steam."

"In a minute." Carey covered the mouthpiece of the receiver with his hand. "I've got the office on the line. They're checking on something for me."

Sabin grinned and shook his head as he saw the scrawled notes on the yellow legal pad on the table beside the phone. "I'm the one who's supposed to be the workaholic. How many times have you told me I should relax when I'm away from the office?"

"This is different." Carey's expression was surprisingly serious. "Did those witnesses identify the make of the car that hit me?"

Sabin's grin vanished. "I haven't called the police yet this morning. Why?"

"Because I think it would be a damn good idea to check. I got bored lying here doing nothing last night and started to add things up. We may not have—" He broke off and spoke into the receiver. "You've got it? Good. Read it to me." He listened, scrawling more notes on the pad in front of him. "Okay. Thanks, Heidi." He hung up the receiver.

"What's this all about, Carey?"

"Call the police." Carey picked up the receiver again and handed it to Sabin. "Then we'll compare notes."

Sabin hesitated, then took the phone and made the call. A few minutes later he hung up. "A Renault. Both witnesses finally agreed on the make."

Carey nodded. "A navy blue Renault." He picked up one of the slips of paper on the bedside table. "A 1989 two-door Renault. License 248J3. It's a rental car, rented at the airport to James Delage."

Sabin stiffened. "What the hell are you saying?"

"I'm saying that my accident had nothing to do with you." Carey paused. "And everything to do with Mallory."

"Mallory?"

"It didn't fit," Carey said. "Delage said Sedikhan Oil refused to pay his wife's expenses to Sedikhan, and it bothered me. You know I can't let something go when it bothers me."

"A bulldog," Sabin agreed, frowning.

"And he wasn't Gregory Peck. He was a very on-edge Anthony Perkins."

"You're not making sense. Tell me."

"He was jealous," Carey said simply. "He saw me in Mallory's trailer and thought I was sleeping with her. He didn't know I was standing in for you. If he'd seen you that night with Mallory, you'd have been the one run over by that Renault."

Sabin felt as if he'd been punched in the stomach. "Lord, you mean Delage . . ."

Carey nodded. "I had Heidi call Sedikhan Oil. They never heard of James Delage." He reached for the legal pad. "And I had her dig up that file that Randolph's Detective Agency sent us. It was just filed away since you said you weren't interested in more than the current information. Delage entered the Markhan Home for the Mentally Ill near Columbus, Ohio, when he was only sixteen. He had stabbed his ex-girlfriend and beaten up her then current boy-friend. The girl lived, and he was released at eighteen—supposedly completely cured." Carey lifted his gaze to meet Sabin's. "He was diagnosed as schizophrenic and extremely violent when he entered the asylum."

Sabin sat down on the edge of the bed. "Lord." His gaze lifted to Carey's. "Ben?"

Carey nodded. "I think it's likely he formed an attachment for Mallory and murdered Ben to free her. Then he came to her rescue by acting as her attorney, but Mallory never saw him as anything but the husband of her friend. He must have been seeth-ing with frustration and jealousy. That's why he made all those telephone calls and hung up when she answered."

"What telephone calls?" Sabin asked sharply.

"Mallory asked me not to tell you." Carey said sheepishly. "She had been receiving nuisance calls ever since Ben died."

"If you'd seen fit to inform me, you might not be in the hospital now," Sabin muttered. "She got a phone call in the middle of the night two days ago. I answered it."

Carey gave a low whistle. "And Delage thought it was me."

Sabin nodded. "He'd never heard my voice before and probably assumed you and Mallory—" He broke off and shot to his feet. "Come on, let's get back to the trailer. Mallory . . ."

Carey tossed the legal pad aside, hopped off the bed and into the wheelchair. "You think she's in danger?"

"Delage killed one man and tried to kill another for her," Sabin said grimly as he pushed the wheelchair toward the door. "How do you think he's going to react when he confronts her with his feelings for her, and she rejects him?"

"James, it's perfectly charming." Mallory peeked over the edge of the balcony extending over the cliff's edge. The light from the bedroom behind her beamed out over the night dark ocean, and she could barely discern the white curl of the surf as it crashed against the rocks two hundred feet below. "And you call this a cottage? The setting reminds me of that seaside mansion in *Rebecca*. I half-expect to see a brooding Mrs. DeWinter lurking somewhere in the background. However did you manage to afford a house like this?"

"I struck it lucky. The previous tenant had an

unexpected death in his family and had to give up his lease and leave suddenly."

"Gerda's station wagon wasn't in the driveway. Where do you suppose she is?"

"Maybe she's communing with nature on the beach." James smiled. "She'll be back all sandy and wind-tossed, swearing at the top of her lungs, because I didn't let her know we were coming today."

"That sounds like her." Poignant loneliness swept through Mallory as she gazed out into the darkness. What was Sabin doing now all those thousands of miles away in Sedikhan?

But she mustn't think about Sabin. It hurt too much. She turned her back on the sea and leaned back on the balcony balustrade to look at James. "You've been wonderful. I know I wasn't very good company on the flight from Marasef."

"You're always good company. You don't have to entertain me, Mallory. I understand you. I'm the only one who does understand you." He turned away. "Just rest and forget all about Litzke while I bring up the luggage. There's a robe in the closet you might like to slip on."

"I'll wait to unpack."

"No!" His voice was so sharp it startled her. "Put on the robe, Mallory. You'll spoil everything if you don't."

"What do you mean?"

The door shut behind James.

She stared at the door. The expression on James face had been . . . strange. Mallory moved slowly across the room and opened the door of the closet.

The robe hanging in the otherwise empty closet was white, filmy, extravagantly lovely, and had a designer label.

"Do you like it?"

Mallory whirled around to face James who was once again standing in the doorway. "You didn't knock."

"I couldn't wait any longer. I knew you wouldn't be able to resist looking at it." He leaned against the doorjamb, a pleased smile on his face. "I had to see your face when you saw my first present to you."

"Present? James that robe cost a great deal of money. I know you and Gerda can't afford—"

"Stop talking about Gerda," he said pettishly. "You know Gerda has nothing to do with this."

Bitter disappointment sank through her as she thought she began to understand. Lord, a pass from James. "Where's Gerda, James?"

"At home. She won't bother us. Don't worry, I took care of everything." He stopped and shook his head. "I tried to talk to her, but she didn't understand."

"Neither do I." Mallory closed the closet door. "But I'm beginning to get a glimmering of what's going on. I paid you your legal fees, James, and I have no intention of giving you a tip in the form of a one-night stand."

"Oh, no," he said softly. "This isn't a one-night stand. This is eternity, Mallory. I've forgiven you for Ben and for Litzke, but now you've got to understand your unfaithfulness must end."

"Litzke?" Mallory felt a chill run down her spine. This was the second time he had mentioned Carey, and she was beginning to suspect something more terrible than she wanted to admit even to herself. "Why are you talking about Carey?"

"I had to punish him, Mallory." James smiled. "No one must ever have you again but me. The first time

Gerda brought you home, I knew you and I were meant to be together."

"No!"

"Yes." James took a step forward, his eyes glittering wildly in his taut face. "I dream of you. You make me dream of you, and then you pretend you don't know. It has to end."

"I never intended . . ." She shook her head dazedly. "You ran Carey down. You could have killed him."

"You made me do it with your infidelity. Just like you made me kill Ben."

She closed her eyes. "Dear Lord, Ben too?"

"I knew you were unhappy. I knew Ben was keeping us from what we could have together."

"James." Her eyes opened, and she tried to speak slowly and clearly. "There is nothing between us. You were only my friend."

"I was your lover. I dreamed it every night. Why do you keep saying—"

"No!" She bolted past him, evading his clutching hand, reaching out to grab her as she passed him. She flew out the door, down the hall, and down the steps.

"Mallory!" James's utterance was a howl of rage. "Stop! Come back to me!"

She could hear his footsteps on the stairs pounding behind her.

"I'll punish you!" James screamed. "Do you think I'll ever let you leave me? We have to be together. You *can't* leave me."

Her breath was coming in harsh, painful gasps as she flew out the front door and ran down the path bordering the cliff. The night was moonless, starless, and she could see nothing in the darkness.

"Mallory!"

He was closer.

She kicked off her high heels and darted toward the edge of the cliff. Perhaps there was a path or—

She collided with a man's solid body. Strong arms closed tightly about her, holding her captive.

She screamed!

"Shh, it's all right."

She struggled wildly, kicking at his shins, trying to get away.

"Mallory, dammit, it's me."

Sabin!

Her knees gave way, and she collapsed against him. "Run! I don't—Sabin . . ." Her hands clutched at his arms. "James. He killed Ben. He's not—"

He smoothed her hair back from her face. "The police have Delage."

"No, he's right behind me."

"If you turn around, you can see the officers taking him to the police car."

"I don't want to turn around." She shuddered, her arms tightening around him as she remembered James's glittering eyes. "I don't want to see him."

"Mallory!" James's voice was shrill with despair. "You can't leave me. We belong together."

Mallory hid her face in Sabin's shoulder.

"I'll kill you! I won't let you leave—"

"Stop him!"

Mallory whirled to see James breaking away from the uniformed policeman holding him.

She froze, gazing at the man running toward her in horror.

"Don't shoot!" Sabin yelled at the policeman. "You'll hit Mallory." He muttered a curse and pushed Mallory behind him as he turned to Delage. "You don't want to kill Mallory. It's me you want, Delage. You made a mistake, it was never Carey. I'm the one who's taking her away from you."

"Mallory!"

Sabin stepped forward as James rushed him, and the edge of his hand knifed down in a karate chop to James's neck that sent him stumbling over the cliff's edge.

James screamed frantically, as he clutched at the air as if it would keep him from falling.

Mallory stared, shocked, unbelieving as he disappeared from view.

She was vaguely conscious of the shouts, of the uniformed men running to the edge of the cliff. "He's gone."

She knew it was an illusion, but she could still hear James screaming her name as he ran after her.

"Come on, Mallory." Sabin gently took her arm. "There's no use in standing here. Let's go to the police car."

"He's dead, isn't he?" she asked dully.

"Probably. It was quite a drop."

"He said it was my fault. He said it was all my fault."

Sabin swore beneath his breath and propelled her toward the police car in the driveway.

"He killed Ben."

"I know."

"He said I made him do it."

"Forget it. He was as nuts as they come. You're practically shell-shocked or you'd realize he wasn't playing with a full deck. We'll talk about it as soon as I can get you to quit shaking."

She hadn't known she was shaking. "We have to find out if he's hurt Gerda. He said she didn't understand. . . ."

"We'll have the police radio for a patrol car to go check out their house and make sure she's safe."

"She's my friend. How am I going to explain?"

"Stop worrying about it." Sabin's voice was rough. "I'll fix it somehow." He opened the rear door of the police car and pushed her onto the backseat. He climbed into the car after her and took her into his arms. He held her close, pushing her cheek into the hollow of his shoulder. "Just stop crying, okay?"

"Okay," she whispered.

Here in the safe refuge of Sabin's arms she could almost believe he could fix everything.

She closed her eyes and clung to him, trying desperately not to remember James's mad, mournful howling of her name as he chased after her along the edge of the cliff.

Ten

"You look much better this morning." Carey looked up from the newspaper to eye Mallory appraisingly as she came into the dining room. "A little fine drawn but at least you don't look like a marble statue on a crypt any longer. I was worried when Sabin brought you back to the apartment last night."

Mallory sat down at the table and reached for the carafe of coffee at her elbow. "I don't remember very much about last night. It was all a horrible blur." She shuddered as she poured coffee into her cup. "Maybe it's better not to dwell on it. The details were pretty ugly. James . . ."

"Sabin said I wasn't to let you get upset again," Carey interrupted. "So I think we'll skip any conversation about Delage. Do you think you could eat some breakfast?"

She shook her head. "Just coffee. Where's Sabin?"

"He drove out to Long Island to see Delage's wife."

"Gerda?" Her grasp tightened on the cup cradled

in her hands. "He told me the police said James hadn't hurt her."

"She's fine," Carey said quickly. "He just wanted to talk to her."

She set the cup down. Her lips twisted. "About me? What can he say? 'I'm sorry Mrs. Delage, but your husband's dead because he wanted to have an affair with your best friend'?"

"No." Carey reached out and covered her hand with his own. "He'll say Delage was unbalanced and formed a fixation that was never at any time encouraged by you."

She shook her head. "It won't help. She *loved* him, Carey. Of course, she's going to blame me."

"Maybe not." He gestured with the arm in the cast to the newspaper he had been reading when she walked into the room. "The rest of the world doesn't."

"No more femme fatale?"

"You're a tragic, romantic heroine. The press is having a field day." He smiled gently. "There hasn't been such a hoopla about anyone since the tabloids tried to turn Jackie into a saint when Kennedy was assassinated."

She shivered. "I could have been the one who died last night if it hadn't been for Sabin." She turned her hand over and returned Carey's clasp. "And you. Sabin told me you were responsible for finding out that James was a murderer."

"My inquiring mind. It's the bane of my existence that things have to fit neatly for me. When Delage struck a sour chord, I had to find out why." He gazed at her soberly. "You could have made things easier for us if you hadn't decided to fly the coop. Sabin was nearly out of his mind when he contacted the security men he had assigned to you and found out you were on your way to the U.S. with Delage. We had no concrete proof yet and hadn't a chance of having the police intercept you at the airport. The only thing Sabin could do was call Randolph and have them meet the plane and follow you to the beach house."

She shivered. "I'm glad you did."

"Our Lear Jet landed thirty minutes after you'd left the airport, and Sabin pulled strings to get the police to assign a black and white to chase after you while Randolph's men radioed directions to us."

She shook her head, tears stinging her eyes. "It was like a nightmare. James was my friend, Carey. You know I'd never encourage him to be anything else."

"I know." He gave her hand a final squeeze before releasing it. "He wasn't sane, Mallory."

"Or perhaps it was me. Maybe I did encourage him in some way."

"Don't be ridiculous."

"What about Ben? He wouldn't have died if—" She set the coffee down, pushed back her chair, and stood up. "I think I'll go and finish packing."

"Packing?" Carey asked, startled.

"I can't stay here forever." Mallory moved toward the door. "Sabin was kind enough to take me in last night, but I mustn't impose any—"

"For Pete's sake, you know Sabin doesn't regard your presence here as an imposition." Carey smiled lopsidedly. "In fact, I'll be lucky he doesn't break my other arm if I let you go before he gets back."

"He won't be angry with you." Mallory looked back at him, her eyes glistening. "He cares about you. You're one of the constants in his life."

"And you're not?"

She shook her head. "You told me yourself. No long-term affairs for Sabin."

"I talk too much. Ask anyone." Carey stood up. "Stay until he gets back and talk to him, Mallory."

"I can't stay. Why do you think I ran away from him before? He told me once I wasn't tough." She smiled tremulously. "I argued with him at the time. I wouldn't argue now. Not where he's concerned."

"Where will you go?"

"I can't tell you." She held up her hand as he started to protest. "You know you'd tell Sabin if I did."

He nodded slowly. "You're right."

"So it's better that I just fade into the sunset." She turned to go. "Good-bye, Carey. I'll miss you. Thanks for everything."

"Oh, no, you don't." Sabin grabbed the suitcase the taxi driver had just placed in the trunk and set it down on the street. "Not this time, Mallory. You're not running away again. Not now. Not ever."

Mallory tensed, bracing herself and then turned to face him. "I'm leaving, Sabin. Please put the suitcase back in the trunk."

"Hell, no." Sabin thrust a bill into the taxi driver's hand. "Take the bags back inside and tell the concierge to send them up to the Wyatt apartment." He didn't wait for an answer. Instead, he took Mallory's arm and propelled her toward the limousine double-parked down the street. "Don't say a word," he said between clenched teeth. "Not a syllable." He opened the rear door and thrust her onto the cushioned seat and climbed in after her. "Just let me sit here and try to get over wanting to strangle you." He motioned for the chauffeur to start the car. "Central Park." He turned to face her. "I couldn't believe it when Carey told me you were just walking out."

"Carey told—" She broke off as she understood. "The car phone. I forgot he could call you."

Sabin's lips set grimly. "No, you thought it safe to run away from me without so much as good-bye."

She looked straight ahead. "I knew you'd be difficult."

"You're damn right I'll be difficult. I'll be more than difficult. I'll be impossible. I was all the way out on Long Island trying to save your friendship with Gerda and you—"

"I could have told you it was hopeless." She looked at him. "Gerda wouldn't listen to you, would she?"

"She listened. I made her listen." Sabin paused. "But she wasn't ready to believe me. I'll have to try again later."

"I didn't think she would. She loved James. It's easier for her to believe I'm to blame for all this than him."

"According to what Carey told me, it's apparently easier for you too." He took her shoulders and shook her. "Listen to me. You were *not* at fault. You did nothing to encourage Delage."

"How do you know?" Her tone was anguished. "How do I know?"

"Because I'm telling you. I know you. You're warm and loving, but only a madman like Delage would mistake friendship for anything deeper." He smiled bitterly. "I had more cause than him, and I never did."

She looked over his shoulder at the traffic passing

by beyond the tinted window. "You once said I was the kind of woman men formed obsessions about."

"You are." He released her shoulders and cradled her cheeks in his hands. "Stop looking out that blasted window and listen to me." His eyes were blazing with intensity as he stared down at her. "You're so damn beautiful, you make me start to shake just looking at you. I told Carey once you were as close as a modern woman could get to Helen of Troy, and I meant it. You're the kind of woman men fight wars over and write great novels about and . . ." He drew a deep breath. "But that's not all you are. You're a decent, intelligent human being, and you deserve the right to choose. You're not to blame if Delage wanted you." He paused. "And you're not to blame, if I love you."

She froze, her gaze on his face. "What?"

"You deserve the right to choose," he repeated hoarsely. "But I have rights too. You weren't fair to me. You didn't give me a chance. You're always running away from me."

"I had to run away."

"Why?" His big hand was oddly clumsy, smoothing her hair away from her face. "You liked the sex. I know you did. And you liked me. I wasn't pushing. Lord, do you know how hard it was for me not to push you? Every moment I was with you I wanted to reach out and grab you and take you back to Kandrahan."

"For three months."

He shook his head. "Forever."

Joy began to sweep through her in a shimmering river. "You said nothing lasted forever."

"I was scared," he said haltingly. "Almost from the

beginning I knew I wasn't going to be able to let you go in three months. But I thought if I tried to hold you that you'd panic. I was afraid you'd go away like all the others. I had to protect myself."

She held her breath. "Why?"

"Because I knew you could destroy me if you went away."

The admission was said with such gruff simplicity, it brought the tears rushing to her eyes. She reached out and clutched at his shoulders. "Shut up. Nothing could destroy you, Sabin. You're the Rock of Gibraltar."

He grimaced in self-disgust. "Just listen to me. One moment I'm telling you that you're not responsible for any of us, and then I try to lay a guilt trip on you." He smiled with an effort. "You're right. I'd survive."

"You bet you would."

"But I wouldn't be happy. My life would be like the summer following your blackberry winter. No matter how beautiful the season, it would be an anticlimax without you." He drew a harsh breath. "So I have a bargain for you."

"Another one?"

He nodded. "This one's very important." He hesitated. "Marry me." He continued in a rush, "I've thought it all out. It could be very beneficial for you. Naturally, I'd guarantee to further your career. I'd cherish and protect you. I wouldn't be the easiest man to live with, but you'd have plenty of money and you wouldn't have to give me a child unless you decided you wanted— "

"Stop."

"It's not enough?"

Her lashes veiled her eyes. "You're overwhelming me. Now, let's see. I get money, a career, protection. What do you get out of this arrangement?"

"You. That's all I want. That's all I've ever wanted from the first moment I saw you."

She turned her head, her lips brushing his palm. "I can't agree to those terms."

He stiffened. "What else can I give you?"

"It's not what you're giving that I object to, but what you're taking." She lifted her gaze to meet his own. "It's not enough. For a brilliant businessman, you're not being very demanding. Now, would you like to hear my terms?"

He became still. "I'm waiting."

"I want you to promise you'll never leave me. If you ever decide you don't love me any longer as a lover, you have to let me be your friend." She reached up and touched the hard line of his jaw. "You have to let me give you at least two children. I'd rather have four, but I'll settle for two." She paused, and a luminous smile lit her face. "And you have to pretend you don't mind when I tell you at least forty times a day how very much I love you."

His eyes widened. "You love—"

She stopped the words with a quick, loving kiss. "Why do you think I ran away, you idiotic man? You wanted to see me act on impulse, to forget about logic and reason. Well, I did that when I ran away from you. I thought it was self-preservation, but I was really in a blind panic because I was afraid of being hurt again."

"I'd never hurt you," he said hoarsely. "I'm not like Ben. You don't have to be afraid."

"Yes, I do. Love is always a risk. The greater the

love, the greater the risk." She laughed shakily. "But it's worth it."

His expression was suddenly wary. "You're sure? You don't have to lie to me. I'll be satisfied with—"

"The devil you will." She chuckled. "You want it all. Do you think I don't know you by now?"

"And you still love me?" A brilliant, joyous smile transformed the rough hardness of his face, making it almost beautiful. "Well, I'll be damned."

"Is it a deal?"

He kissed her hard, hot, and sweet. "No."

She looked at him in surprise. "No?"

"Stop the car," he ordered the chauffeur. "Pull up beside one of those hansom cabs across from the park." He grabbed her hand while he opened the door as the limousine stopped at the curb. "Come on."

"Where are we going?"

He pulled her toward a vacant carriage waiting at the curb. "No more deals."

He lifted her into the carriage and climbed in after her. "When our grandchildren ask where we were when I proposed to you, I want you to be able to tell them I did it right. A man has to do these things with panache when he's paying suit to Helen of Troy." He motioned toward the driver, and the gray horse clopped past the Plaza Hotel toward Central Park. "So forget about bargains and deals. This is the real thing."

She had never seen Sabin's expression so boyish or full of joy, Mallory thought lovingly, as she leaned back in the carriage and laced her fingers through his. The breeze gently touched her cheeks and tugged at her hair as the carriage entered the verdant haven of the park.

She knew there was no wrong way for them to seal their vows if it meant they were going to go through life together, but if Sabin felt better about this romantic gesture how could she argue? He was actually speaking of a future stretching into forever and forming the strong roots of home and family.

She nestled contentedly closer to him. "You're absolutely right," she said solemnly. "By all means, we have to consider the grandchildren."

THE EDITOR'S CORNER

We suspect that Cupid comes to visit our Bantam offices every year when we're preparing the Valentine's Day books. It seems we're always specially inspired by the one exclusively romantic holiday in the year. And our covers next month reflect just how inspired we were . . . by our authors who also must have had a visit from the chubby cherub. They shimmer with cherry-red metallic ink and are presents in and of themselves—as are the stories within. They range from naughty to very nice!

First, we bring you Suzanne Forster's marvelous **WILD CHILD**, LOVESWEPT #384. Cat D'Angelo had been the town's bad girl and Blake Wheeler its golden boy when the young assistant D.A. had sent her to the reformatory for suspected car theft. Now, ten years later, she has returned to work as a counselor to troubled kids—and to even the score with the man who had hurt her so deeply! Time had only strengthened the powerful forces that drew them together . . . and Blake felt inescapable hunger for the beautiful, complicated hellcat who could drive a man to ruin—or to ecstasy. Could the love and hate Cat had held so long in her heart be fused by the fire of mutual need and finally healed by passion? We think you'll find **WILD CHILD** delicious—yet calorie free—as chocolates packaged in a red satin box!

Treat yourself to a big bouquet with Gail Douglas's *The Dreamweavers:* **BEWITCHING LADY,** LOVESWEPT #385. When the Brawny Josh Campbell who looked as if he could wield a sword as powerfully as any clansman stopped on a deserted road to give her a ride, Heather Sinclair played a mischievous Scottish lass to the hilt, beguiling the moody but fascinating man whose gaze hid inner demons . . . and hinted at a dangerous passion she'd never known. Josh felt his depression lift after months of despair, but he was too cynical to succumb to this delectable minx's appeal . . . or was he? A true delight!

Sweet, fresh-baked goodies galore are yours in Joan
(continued)

Elliott Pickart's **MIXED SIGNALS**, LOVESWEPT #386. Katha Logan threw herself into Vince Santini's arms, determined to rescue the rugged ex-cop from the throng of reporters outside city hall. Vince enjoyed being kidnapped by this lovely and enchanting nut who drove like a madwoman and intrigued him with her story of a crime he just *had* to investigate . . . with her as his partner! Vince believed that a man who risked his life for a living had no business falling in love. Katha knew she could cherish Vince forever if he'd let her, but playing lovers' games wasn't enough anymore. Could they learn to fly with the angels and together let their passions soar?

We give a warm, warm greeting—covered with hearts, with flowers—to a new LOVESWEPT author, but one who's not new to any of us who treasure romances. Welcome Lori Copeland, who brings us LOVESWEPT #387, **DARLING DECEIVER,** next month. Bestselling mystery writer Shae Malone returned to the sleepy town where he'd spent much of his childhood to finish his new novel, but instead of peace and quiet, he found his home invaded by a menagerie of zoo animals temporarily living next door . . . with gorgeously grown-up Harriet Whitlock! As a teenager she'd chased him relentlessly, embarrassed him with poems declaring everlasting love, but now she was an exquisite woman whose long-legged body made him burn with white-hot fire. Harri still wanted Shae with shameless abandon, but did she dare risk giving her heart again?

Your temperature may rise when you read **HEART-THROB** by Doris Parmett, LOVESWEPT #388. Hannah Morgan was bright, eager, beautiful—an enigma who filled television director Zack Matthews with impatience . . . and a sizzling hunger. The reporter in him wanted to uncover her mysteries, while the man simply wanted to gaze at her in moonlight. Hannah was prepared to work as hard as she needed to satisfy the workaholic heartbreaker . . . until her impossibly virile boss crumbled her defenses with tenderness and ignited a hunger she'd never expected to feel again. Was she

(continued)

willing to fight to keep her man? Don't miss this sparkling jewel of a love story. A true Valentine's Day present.

For a great finish to a special month, don't miss Judy Gill's **STARGAZER**, LOVESWEPT #389, a romance that shines with the message of the power of love . . . at any age. As the helicopter hovered above her, Kathy M'Gonigle gazed with wonder at her heroic rescuer, but stormy-eyed Gabe Fowler was furious at how close she'd come to drowning in the sudden flood—and shocked at the joy he felt at touching her again! Years before, he'd made her burn with desire, but she'd been too young and he too restless to settle down. Now destiny had brought them both home. Could the man who put the stars in her eyes conquer the past and promise her forever?

All our books—well, their authors wish they could promise you forever. That's not possible, but authors and staff can wish you wonderful romance reading.

Now it is my great pleasure to give you one more Valentine's gift—namely, to reintroduce you to our Susann Brailey, now Senior Editor, who will grace these pages in the future with her fresh and enthusiastic words. But don't think for a minute that you're getting rid of me! I'll be here—along with the rest of the staff—doing the very best to bring you wonderful love stories all year long.

As I have told you many times in the past, I wish you peace, joy, and the best of all things—the love of family and friends.

Carolyn Nichols

Carolyn Nichols
Editor
LOVESWEPT
Bantam Books
666 Fifth Avenue
New York, NY 10103

FAN OF THE MONTH

Joni Clayton

It's really great fun to be a LOVESWEPT Fan of the Month as it provides me with the opportunity to publicly thank Carolyn Nichols, Bantam Books, and some of my favorite authors: Sandra Brown, Iris Johansen, Kay Hooper, Fayrene Preston, Helen Mittermeyer and Deborah Smith (to name only a few!).

My good friend, Mary, first introduced me to romance fiction and LOVESWEPTS in 1984 as an escape from the pressures of my job. Almost immediately my associates noticed the difference in my disposition and attitude and questioned the reason for the change. They all wanted to thank LOVESWEPT!

It did not take me long to discover that most romance series were inconsistent in quality and were not always to my liking—but not LOVESWEPT. I have thoroughly enjoyed each and every volume. All were "keepers" . . . so of course I wanted to own the entire series. I enlisted the aid of friends and used book dealers. Presto! The series was complete! As soon as LOVESWEPT was offered through the mail, I subscribed and have never missed a copy!

I have since retired from the "hurly-burly" of the working world and finally have the time to start to reread all of my LOVESWEPT "keepers."

To Carolyn, all of the authors, and the LOVESWEPT staff—Thanks for making my retirement so enjoyable!

60 Minutes to a Better, More Beautiful You!

Now it's easier than ever to awaken your sensuality, stay slim forever—even make yourself irresistible. With Bantam's bestselling subliminal audio tapes, you're only 60 minutes away from a better, more beautiful you!

__ 45004-2	**Slim Forever**	$8.95
__ 45112-X	**Awaken Your Sensuality**	$7.95
__ 45081-6	**You're Irresistible**	$7.95
__ 45035-2	**Stop Smoking Forever**	$8.95
__ 45130-8	**Develop Your Intuition**	$7.95
__ 45022-0	**Positively Change Your Life**	$8.95
__ 45154-5	**Get What You Want**	$7.95
__ 45041-7	**Stress Free Forever**	$7.95
__ 45106-5	**Get a Good Night's Sleep**	$7.95
__ 45094-8	**Improve Your Concentration**	$7.95
__ 45172-3	**Develop A Perfect Memory**	$8.95

Bantam Books, Dept. LT, 414 East Golf Road, Des Plaines, IL 60016

Please send me the items I have checked above. I am enclosing $_____ (please add $2.00 to cover postage and handling). Send check or money order, no cash or C.O.D.s please. (Tape offer good in USA only.)

Mr/Ms _____

Address _____

City/State _____ Zip _____

LT-12/89

Please allow four to six weeks for delivery.
Prices and availability subject to change without notice.

NEW!
Handsome Book Covers Specially Designed To Fit Loveswept Books

Our new French Calf Vinyl book covers come in a set of three great colors—royal blue, scarlet red and kachina green.

Each 7" × 9½" book cover has two deep vertical pockets, a handy sewn-in bookmark, and is soil and scratch resistant.

To order your set, use the form below.